# Feast
## of the
# Raven

# Feast
# of the
# Raven

WULFHEDINN: BOOK ONE

## CATHERINE SPADER

**Feast of the Raven**
Published by Quillstone Press
Littleton, CO

Library of Congress Control Number: 2015960642

Spader, Catherine, Author
**Feast of the Raven**
Catherine Spader

ISBN: 978-0-9971535-0-7
Cover design by Nick Zelinger at NZ Graphics

Fantasy / Historical

QUANTITY PURCHASES: Schools, companies, professional groups, clubs, and other organizations may qualify for special terms when ordering quantities of this title. For information, email info@quillstonepress. com.

Littleton, CO

For my Dad, Henry Meier

In memory of treasured times we shared
discussing medieval history
and exploring ruins and castles

# Acknowledgments

Most special thanks to my husband Craig Spader, whose love and faith in me has never faltered. I could not have done this without you.

Humble gratitude to my mentors: My mom Shirley Meier, who shared her love of writing and literature; James Hallman, a visionary, egalitarian editor who tolerated a lot but accepted nothing but the best; Linda Sweeney, my writing teacher and the first one to see my vision of history, myth, and lore; Sam Ostrin, for his gems of wisdom on writing and photography, given in a manner only he could provide; and Janet Boivin, who took a giant leap of faith and hired me as a writer based only on my unpublished short story.

Thanks also to my writing friends, rogue warriors who labored many hours to provide precious feedback: Amanda Langdon, best Medieval friend forever; Corrine Cook, goddess of all things mythology; Christie Hartman, publishing super-hero; James Stage, understated, edgy genius; Mike Weldon, sword swinging champion of driving home a good point; Nick Stasnopolis, military history guru—although he is still wrong about the battle of the Teutoburg Forest.

…with a deep appreciation for the music of Jethro Tull, which has enchanted and inspired me for more than four decades.

# Europe
782 AD

Danes

Saxons
.Raven's Stones
.Paderborn and Lippespringe

The Frankish Kingdom

# Wulfhedinn

## 782 AD - Saxony, Germania

*Far away, a wolf howls*
*Silence*
*Nothing but black night*
*It calls again, a longer wail, distant and isolated*
*Then silence*
*Night deepens*

Voices broke the stillness—the sounds of soldiers eating together, drinking together…laughing.

I watched them from a perch in a tree overlooking the wall. Their fires glowed with warmth, the smoke rising over the wall toward me. It stung my nose and burned my eyes, wafting across the river that divided the King's bright garrison from the dark forest where I dwelt. Alone.

*The howling draws closer*
*An aching, lonely call*
*Searching*
*…unanswered*

*Hairs bristle on the back of my neck*
*It returns to me*
*A hollow echo*
*…unanswered*

*Creeping softly*
*Coming closer*
*Growing louder*
*…until a deafening cry*

I should have resisted, but the wolf skin was the only soft thing that had touched me in a long time. I pulled it close and raised the hood, masking my face.

*Its beating heart steals inside me*
*Peering through the eyes of the beast*
*…pounding harder and harder*
*Muscles surge*
*Strength rules*

I watched King Karl's army encampment with a keen wolf's eye. In the center, his huge tent glowed like an emerald. The wall surrounding the garrison was built of stout timbers, and the forest had been cleared away from most of it. Guards paced at the top and torches lit the wall, leaving little area that was dark and unprotected.

After several hours, the guards loosened their grips on their weapons. Their expressions grew flat and several yawned, unmindful and ready to be relieved of duty. They felt safe from the rebel Saxons atop their palisade, but I would not risk breeching the wall by myself, even as Wulfhedinn. There were better ways to get inside.

Soon the monk came along, trotting up the path toward the gate as he did most nights. His tonsured hair was dripping from his bath in the nearby sacred spring. He was naked, except for the cross hanging around his neck. His habit was draped over his arm, dragging in the dirt. He mumbled to himself and stepped lightly down the well-worn path back to his people, his place. Smiling, his wet face gleamed with God's blessing.

*A deafening wail*
*For what I am denied*

I jumped down from the tree, blocking his way, and raised my long axe. He reacted like lightning. Dropping his clothing, he pulled a long seax he had hidden underneath. His grip on the blade was quick and sure.

I paused, reconsidering this man of God. I did not expect him to fight back, so I swung at him with the butt of the axe. He blocked the blow with his seax but was knocked down and dropped it. I stepped on his chest and held the axe edge against his throat.

His eyes flashed. He fumbled for his cross and thrust it between us.

"Wulfhedinn! Stand Back!" His throat quivered. "God, deliver me from the jaws of the demon wolf warrior!"

*The hood falls*
*The beast retreats into the forest*
*A remote yowl...*
*Fading*
*Fading...*
*But never far*

The monk studied my face as I did his. Someone in his past had crushed his nose and left him with a warped forehead.

He saw my hesitation, and his hand stopped trembling. "These crooked eyes see more than you know, Wulfhedinn," he said. "I see the hatred in your soul; the deep loathing of me, of all Christians...but you must let me live! God tells me it is not my time yet."

"You will live," I said.

His raised a twisted brow. "What, then, do you want of me?"

"The Holy Spear."

He cackled like an old woman, a strange sound from a man who could handle a seax.

"The Holy Spear?! Do I look like the King? *I* do not possess the most powerful holy relic in the kingdom."

"I have watched you," I said. "You mingle with army officers and court officials and are esteemed at court. You come and go through the gate of the garrison without question. You can take me to it."

"Impossible." He squirmed under my foot, grabbing my leg. "The King rarely lets it out of his sight, and then it is guarded by a dozen of his best soldiers."

"Find a way." I leaned on his ribs and hefted my axe, aiming at this throat.

He groaned and released my leg.

*A sharp wind kicks up*
*Scream piercing the dark sky*
*She comes*
*The Raven, black as night*
*Plunging close to the monk*
*Veers up and perches in a tree*
*Budding branches chant softly in the wind*
*She ruffles her oily black feathers and calls to me*

*I hunger*

*Wild eyes feast*
*White throat…open, vulnerable*
*Heart pounding*
*Jaws stinging*
*The pleasure of warm blood*

*Feed the wolf*
*Feed the Raven*

My axe hung motionless, poised to fall.

"No! By God's will," the monk pleaded. "I shall take you to the spear…"

*The beast disappears into the forest*
*The Raven screeching*
*…follows it into darkness*

I kicked him over. He stood slowly, rubbing his chest with a glower on his crooked face. He made no effort to cover himself, eying his seax on the ground.

I snatched it up. "You cannot escape me."

He sighed. "No, I am not quite the fool I appear to be. I will take you to the Holy Spear, but I warn you that stealing it is futile. It is a *Christian* relic. It will have no power in the hands of your heathen people or your rebel leader, Widukind."

"I have no leader—and no people."

"Not a Saxon wolf warrior, one of the Wulfhednar? Who… what…?"

More questions I did not want to answer formed on his lips. I bared my teeth and snarled.

He recoiled. "Yes! Yes! We will go, but I must consult with God first." He folded his hands around his cross and looked to the sky, murmuring. "Yes, My Lord…I will," he said. "You are truly blessed, Wulfhedinn. It is the Lord's wish that I take you to the Holy Spear, but I must think more on this…think with God's mind, hear God's plan." He scratched his ragged wet tonsure. "I cannot parade you through the middle of a Frankish garrison like *that*. There is too much talk—and fear—of wolf warriors now."

"Think quickly," I said, nodding toward his clothing on the ground. "And get dressed."

He opened his arms, reaching toward the sky. "God has given me His power. I need nothing else."

He began pacing back and forth, muttering to himself with every turn of his heel. He raised a finger and shouted, "Amen! God has shown me the way."

"What way is that?"

He picked up his cloak and tossed it to me. "First, you must take off that foul hide and wear this."

I ignored him and threw his cloak over the top of my wolf skin. The wool smelled of incense, stale beer, and old blood—

goat's blood, like a butcher. I wrinkled my nose at the foul combination. How is this the same man who washed his body every day?

"I must get close enough to touch the spear," I said.

"Ha!" He frowned as he put on his tunic and cowl. "You ask for much. *Everyone* wants to touch the Holy Spear." He crossed his arms and thought a moment and grinned. "...but God tells me that you will be one of the few to hold it. I just might be able to sneak you in during the assembly."

"Do it then." I drew his cloak around my shoulders, trying to keep my cross hidden, but it slipped out. It rattled against the bones that hung with it on a leather cord around my neck. I fumbled to tuck it under the cloak, but the monk had seen it.

"Blessed Mother of God!" He crossed himself. "My Lord's cross, strung with flesh and bones, ears and noses! What sort of beast *are* you?"

I shoved him toward the garrison with the axe handle. "A beast that is damned."

# Fight for God

The monk walked, rubbing his sore shoulder. "Where would you get a long axe like that?" he asked. "Such fine forged steel...that is no farmer's tool for chopping wood—a deadly weapon. And the throwing axe in your belt—the best kind of Frankish francisca—all quite grand for someone who does not wear shoes."

"I hate shoes."

"Indeed. You care for your weapons far better than yourself."

I pushed him forward. "Shut your mouth and keep moving."

In a few minutes, we arrived at the river bank. I pulled him behind a large tree to stay concealed. A contingent of soldiers marched up the road toward the gate—a heavily armored horseman, his bannerman, and several dozen foot soldiers.

"The camp has grown much today," the monk whispered. "Noble Scola riders and thousands of infantrymen. The lords come from the far reaches of the Frankish kingdom to the King's general assembly to proclaim their devotion to God, King Karl, and the Holy Spear—and more are on the way."

The soldiers moved slowly, fatigued from a long march. They passed our hiding spot then forded the shallow river. At the gate, the guards stopped and questioned them.

"The King is taking no chances," the monk said. "There are rumors that rebel Saxons are nearby, so he has doubled the watch. The gate is too risky; they will stop me once they see you. We must go another way, a secret way—upriver."

"Monk, if you lead me astray..."

"I will not, as God is my witness." He pointed to the sky. "I cannot die yet. I have much to do to atone for my sins."

As we followed the river to the northeast, I wondered what kind of sins this mad monk could have committed. I had known holy men who were pious and those that were wicked, but he was unlike any of them.

He started talking again. "Are you wearing the flesh and bones of Christians you have killed around your neck?"

I kept silent, but he persisted. "Will you add my ear or finger to your demented string of prayer beads?"

"Just your tongue. You talk too much."

That silenced him but not for long.

"Who *are* you?" he asked. "You look like a heathen Saxon, yet your accent sounds like that of a Christian Frank."

"I am both—and neither."

He was wordless, but I knew his mind was churning. The strange monk would soon be muttering again.

We continued upriver until it narrowed, and the ground became cool and moist under my feet.

*Soft light filters through the budding tree branches*
*The monk's face glows with it*
*Radiant blue funnel, flowing with sacred waters*
*It reflects everything*
*Sees everything*
*Eye of Wodan*

He was leading me to the spring where he had bathed.

I stopped. "We must go around it."

"What? The spring?" He cackled. "You are a strange demon, fearing the heathen spring. It is quite safe, I assure you."

"Wodan dwells there…"

"But you are one of his wolf warriors, are you not?"

"No."

"No?" He tilted his head. "I still do not understand…"

"We must go another way."

"You need not fear the Eye. I revere all that is sacred, including the wild heathen places. Wodan accepts me there."

"You speak of madness, monk."

"No, of reason. I have made amends with the heathen god for the actions of King Karl. The King considers the spring as his own, but he does not understand that no man can own a sacred place. He has desecrated it, changing the name to Lippespringe and using it to wash the filth off his foul courtiers."

"*You* swam there."

"With respect, performing proper rite and ceremony."

"I will not go near it and would never bath there."

He wrinkled his brow and scanned me from head to toe. Smirking, he clearly believed that I did not wash at all.

I scratched my beard, knotted with leaves and dirt. "Enough, monk." I shoved him forward. "Keep moving—away from the spring, beyond the light of the Eye."

"Detouring that far around it will take an hour or more, and we will have to travel deeper into the Saxon forest. It is full of bandits."

"We will risk it."

We continued on an untracked route, taking a wide diversion around the spring.

*The light follows*
*It watches…*
*Fading slowly as we walk*
*…disappearing*

The monk began mumbling. At first, he garbled his words, but he repeated them like a chant until they became clear.

"Flesh and bones…flesh and bones…pieces of the dead… flesh and bones. Who do you wear around your neck, Wulfhedinn? I hope they were deserving of death."

"The bones of saints—and I did not kill for them!" I quickly regretted answering him.

"Relics of Christian saints. How would *you* get such things? What do you do with them? Offer them to the pagan gods?"

"I am no pagan."

"You are *Christian?*"

"Be silent," I whispered.

The woodland had gone quiet. Mice no longer scampered through rotting leaves, and moles had stopped tunneling below my feet. I smelled three men lurking in the brush, lying in wait.

A twig snapped to my right. Footsteps stumbled through the brush. Someone tripped and fell with a groan. The monk darted into the brush like a startled rabbit.

I dropped the cloak he had given me and pulled the wolf hood low over my face.

*Crouching low on hind legs*
*Its pulse my own*
*...pounding...pounding...pounding*
*Its rage my own*

A club swung at me. My long axe knocked it from the attacker's hand. I struck at his neck and cleaved bone, separating it from sinew. His head fell next to his body, showering me in a bloody mist.

*Warming me*
*Quickens my heart*
*Scent of death filling the wood*

Another attacker leapt with a seax. I swung around. My axe sank into his ribs, crushing bone. He crashed to the ground, gurgling as he clawed at his gaping chest. Another swing at his neck—beheaded as swiftly as the first.

I turned away, but it was too late—I had seen their faces.

*The Raven screams above*
*Following in my wake*

I hacked and chopped at their skulls until they shattered and were pounded into pulp.

It made no difference—they had seen me.

*Where the Raven looms*
*Tonight she feeds well*
*On my sin*
*My soul*

I ran through the brush to the third attacker, but the monk was already there. He stood over him, bloody dagger in hand, a slash running from ear to ear.

He fell to his knees, babbling and lamenting, "Oh, my Lord...my Lord God!"

The attacker was still alive, gasping and choking on his own blood. The monk put his trembling hands over the wound, trying futilely to stop the bleeding.

"Get away, monk. He is dead."

I raised my axe, and the monk deftly rolled out of the way. One chop and the head rolled, its eyes staring at me then up at the sky.

*Where the Raven looms*

The monk made the sign of the cross, his eyes gaping. "I have never seen anyone behead a man with one swing," he said. "Truly, God has not damned you, Wulfhedinn. He has blessed you with great strength."

"*Blessed* me?"

*A growl*
*Rising from deep within the chest*
*From the heart*
*Pain and wrath*

I split the skull in half and swung again. It could not remain intact, to look at me, to see.

"Stop!" The monk stood and held up a hand. "This will not undo that which has been done."

My axe stopped in midair.

*The beast disappears into the forest*
*The Raven screeching*
*...follows it into darkness*

"No man of God has ever stopped me," I said, pulling off the wolf hood. "Who *are* you, monk?"

He straightened his back, squaring his shoulders. "I am Brother Pyttel, monk and ordained priest, assistant to Alcuin, the King's utmost advisor and educator of the court. I hear God...and the King listens."

"Most monks do not know how to slit a man's throat. Where did you learn to fight?"

"In my youth, I was a fair soldier." His gaze grew distant, and his shoulders sagged. "But it did not feel the way I thought it would. I got used to the long campaigns, to hunger, to the cold and wet, but I could not get used to...I will never be the man I was before that...my killing time is over, I tell you."

He frowned at the attacker at our feet. The man was armed with a simple club. He wore a threadbare tunic, and his bony feet were battered.

The monk began to pace, rubbing his bloody dagger vigorously on his habit. "It is over, I tell you!" His voice rose. "Yes, My Lord, yes! You have given me your power now."

He rubbed and rubbed until I thought the steel would wear thin. When it was clean enough for him, he sheathed it.

"I now serve God's chosen King on earth, King Karl," he said. "I am dedicated to converting the heathen barbarian Saxons to Christianity. I have been all over their lands building churches, preaching God's word…it is over, I tell you, my killing time." He made the sign of the cross. "Yes, my Lord, I will."

I cleaned my axes on the grass and wiped them on my breeches until the monk smirked at me. My polishing was nearly as hearty as his. He chuckled and picked up the dead man, grunting with the awkward load. Blood poured from the neck, drenching him.

"What are you doing?" I asked. "We must go…"

"We cannot linger to bury them, but I can bring them together for a blessing. Carry his head for me."

"Leave it," I said.

"I must do this. You will have to kill me to stop me."

I could not raise a weapon to him, this monk who killed like a warrior and drove away the wolf—yet had done me no harm. I glared at him instead.

He shivered, stumbled, and dropped the body. "Such demon eyes you have! It would do your condemned soul good to help me—if indeed you are a Christian."

I could not bear to touch the head, so I picked up the body. "You take the head."

He scooped up the pieces of the skull and pieced them back together, soaking himself in more blood.

"Yes, yes, this will do your soul good," he repeated. "Did you notice? They are Christian." He picked a cross out of the mud, nearly dropping the head. We carried the man to where the other attackers lay.

He gasped. "What more wickedness have you done, Wulfhedinn?"

"Be silent!" I laid the man down next to the others and turned away.

*Faces linger*
*Seeing everything*

Their bodies were small and thin. Barely more than boys, they were as ragged and poorly armed as the older man. Their smashed faces were unrecognizable now, but they had shared the fair hair and round faces of the Saxon tribes. They had resembled each other and were probably kin, father and sons. A wife and other children likely waited at home for their return. More things the wolf had not noticed.

Brother Pyttel placed the cross on the man's chest. "Starving Saxon peasants. Many of these farmers on the borderlands have lost everything in the King's campaigns—even the ones who converted to Christianity. They now survive by attacking those who wander into the Teutoburg Forest. The woods are thick with these farmer bandits."

*The Raven dives from the dark sky*
*Alighting on the father*
*Another dead*
*Slain by the wolf*
*...by my own hand*
*Their blood drying on my body*
*Marking me*

*Blood stained beak*
*She drinks her fill and flies away*
*Red eyes fade into night*

*Vanishing with the souls she carries*
*Quenched…never satisfied*

*Bring me more, Wulfhedinn*

The monk's gaze followed mine to the sky. "What do you see?" he asked.

I shook my head.

He shrugged his shoulders, knelt, and held his hands over the bodies. "Lord God, forgive these peasants for their folly. Bring them into your Kingdom of Heaven. Amen." He stood, his face grave. "Do you not pray?"

"No…not anymore."

He frowned and wandered a few steps away.

"Where are you going?" I asked.

He stopped at a pool of stagnant water. "We must wash… because it is over…over…"

He waded into the pool and dunked his head. When he came up for air, he was staring into nowhere, then he plunged into the murky water and stayed under longer than I could hold my own breath. I waded in to pull him out, but he jumped up, coughing and gasping for air.

"Move on," I said, keeping my long axe in hand.

He stumbled out of the water and mumbled, "…is over… is over."

I hardened my heart and steadied my sight forward. We continued through the forest, following a narrow animal track.

"How much farther?" I asked.

"We are about half way there," he said.

Our path soon became overgrown with thickets, and we had to pick our way slowly through the thorny branches.

"Is there no better way?" I snapped.

"Not if you want to remain hidden," Brother Pyttel said, freeing his habit slowly from the thorns. "You remind me of a story—a tale that Frankish mothers tell their children to keep them from wandering into the woodland. They talk of a troubled boy, a bastard...born the son of a Frankish woman who was raped by a Saxon Wulfhedinn, a demon wolf warrior."

*The wolf aches, his call carries pain...*
*Far...yet so near*
*Alone in his grief*

I could not stand to hear it, to feel it again. "Shut your mouth."

He persisted, speaking rapidly. "His mother baptized the boy a Christian, but that did not drive out his father's beast. She sent him to the monastery to shield him from the demon, but the boy defied God and embraced the wolf spirit, invoking it with magic to give him the strength and fury of no other. They say he even killed a monk..."

I grabbed him and threw him into the thorn bush. "No more!"

He winced but continued. "...they called him demon seed. They excommunicated him from the church and banished him into the wilds—a lone wolf that haunts the woodlands to this day."

A few tiny drops of his blood dripped from scratches made by the thorns. I grabbed him by the throat. A single swing of the axe would silence him, end it.

*Poised low on haunches, scruff raised…*
*Ready to attack*
*Kill him*
*Release the rage*

*The Raven lurks above*
*Screaming for his blood*

*Feed the wolf*
*Feed the Raven*

"Will the beast kill another monk, or will he return to God?" he gasped.

I released his throat and threw him down. He rolled onto the ground, coughing.

"Fight for God!" he cried, his eyes darting.

"What? What are you saying, monk?"

"The spear will not give you what you seek."

"What would you know of it?"

"Have *any* of those relics hanging around your neck given you peace?"

My blood cooled as I fingered each ear, nose, and bone.

"Relics will not protect you from the beast," he said, "and they will not save your soul." He measured his words, speaking clearly. "You cannot invoke God with magic. Grace dwells not in the spear, but in the deed. Relics can only inspire the deed. You must fight for your soul."

Fight for my soul? What did he mean? The monk was mad enough to confront me with my past but was also cunning and clever—perhaps too clever.

"Fight for King Karl," he said.

"I fight for no king."

"God's chosen King, the holder of the Holy Spear," he said. "King Karl has united most of the kingdoms north of Rome in Christianity, but he has failed to bring all of the pagan Saxons to God. Spirits roam in their forests. The old gods still rule. There are rumors that the rebel pagans are raising an army of Wulfhednar—undefeatable wolf warriors, like you." He scratched his chin. "The King cannot defeat them with mortal soldiers alone. He needs a demon to conquer demons. He needs you."

I glared at him. "Why should I fight for him? What will it do for me?"

"Far more than the Holy Spear can do. Loyalty to King Karl is loyalty to God—the promise of heavenly grace."

I grappled with the idea. "Why should I trust you?"

"Because my sins are as great as yours." He sighed and paused. "What is your real name, Wulfhedinn?"

I hesitated. No one had asked in many years.

"You cannot exist without a name."

"I don't exist."

He frowned. "A man must have a name—even a man who has been banished."

"Gerwulf," I said.

"Gerwulf," he repeated. "You must fight, Gerwulf. You certainly know how to do *that*. You have fought and killed to damn your soul. Will you not do as much to save it?"

He did not let me answer. "Good," he said. "You may save us both."

# Power Over Man and Beast

⁓⁓

**S**moke burned my nose as we neared the garrison wall. It hung in the air, thick with ash and the stink of smoldering campfires, torches, and midden piles. I breathed through my mouth but could not escape the stifling smell.

The monk took me to a place where the brush grew up against the wall, and we could approach it without being seen by the guard. I scanned the stout timbers, three times my height.

*The Raven waits there, perched on top*
*Return to the wilds, Wulfhedinn*
*Go back...*

*Ash was filling my lungs. My throat tightened.*

*...and she flies back into the forest*

A drum began to beat, calling me in different direction. It beckoned from behind the wall—a lively tune. It did not threaten like a call to war; it danced.

"The garrison is feasting and celebrating the general assembly," said Brother Pyttel. "It is a good time to slip through camp. Many of the soldiers have gone to the camp followers' sector, and the King's defense is not as solid as it appears." He winked and shifted a loose timber, revealing a gap large enough to squeeze through. "An escape route for the King, although he will not use it. King Karl does not run."

I peeked through the gap at a large stack of firewood.

"It is well hidden," he said. "No one will see our entrance. Follow me, and I will do the talking if we are stopped."

I threw the monk's cloak over my head, hiding as much of my face as possible. We squeezed through the hole, and he shifted the timber back into place.

Voices approached, and we ducked low behind the firewood. A flickering torch threw three shadows against the wall—two men and a woman. They drew nearer, stumbled, laughed, and passed our hiding spot.

We slipped from behind the firewood and moved quietly through rows of soldiers' tents. They formed a defensive circle around the larger, finer shelters of noblemen. King Karl's assembly hall towered over it all—a palace of a tent. On the wall, the letters KRLS were embroidered in gold and placed on the four points of a cross. In the middle of the cross were the letters a, o, and u.

"Karolus," I muttered.

Brother Pyttel turned. "What...?"

"The King flaunts his Latin name yet makes a riddle of it."

The monk raised a brow. "You can read that?"

"I was educated in a monastery—for a time." Why had I told him?

A trace of a smile crossed his lips, but for once, he kept quiet.

We moved on, skirting a campfire where a few soldiers gathered. From the far side of camp, the drum played. A flute joined in, and drunken laughter floated across the night air—as did the stink of horse shit.

"We are too close to the stables," I said. "Noblemen's horses will be heavily guarded."

"Agreed," said Brother Pyttel.

He turned to take a different route, but my scent had already spooked the horses. They snorted and whinnied, and the stable boys called to each other to calm them. Suddenly, several guards appeared in our path. They were unarmored foot soldiers equipped with battered wooden shields and simple iron spears.

"Name your business," one of them demanded.

"I am Brother Pyttel, in the service of Alcuin, scholar and advisor to King Karl. The King awaits us."

"Yes, the King's monk. The lunatic," the guard said, tilting his head, trying to see my face. "But who is this?" He flipped my hood back with the tip of his spear.

I gripped my axe under the cloak, ready to strike.

"This is my holy brother," said Brother Pyttel. "He is here to aid me in the conversion of the Saxons."

The guard considered me from head to toe. He smelled of stale beer and old piss. "He looks more like a bloody animal than a monk."

I would have killed him before he could utter another word, but Brother Pyttel put a calm arm around my shoulders. "He has been in the wilds for a long time—to pray and get closer to God," he said.

The other guards, who smelled as foul as the first, scoffed.

"Why are you covered with blood?" the first guard asked.

"An accident…a hunting accident," said Brother Pyttel. "My brother had not eaten in a while."

His answer raised more questions than it answered, but the guard snorted, spit and let us pass.

We soon reached the King's assembly hall, a massive tent of emerald green. A crowd packed the large canopied entrance. They craned their necks to see inside. A commanding voice spoke, and the crowd murmured. The smoky air was thick with tension.

Heavily armed Scola soldiers were posted all around the hall. They were better outfitted than any other soldiers I had seen in camp. Their thick muscular arms held spears and shields bearing the King's insignia. Matching chainmail hauberks protected their broad chests, and Frankish long swords were sheathed at their sides. The Scola were well-known as skilled fighters on foot or horseback—the deadliest of the Frankish troops. I could not fight them in their own camp if I was discovered.

Brother Pyttel sensed my unease. "They know me well. They will not bother us."

Their expressions remained stone-like as we passed, as if they were accustomed to the monk's appearance. We passed unimpeded into the tent's rear entrance and entered a large antechamber.

The room reeked of rotting flesh. I recognized it instantly—raw wolf hides. Flies hovered and droned around masses of fur that were stacked to the ceiling—a storeroom of death.

*The droning grows into wailing*
*…yelping…*
*Leg crushed in a steel trap*
*…thrashing…snarling…*
*Spears stab though ribs*
*Jabbing…tearing, twisting*
*Peeling hide, searing flesh*
*The anguish piled all around me*
*Within me*

I grabbed the monk by the collar, lifting him off his feet. "I will not become another hide in the King's collection."

"As God is my witness, I swear…" he gasped, the stitches in his habit tearing. "I have not deceived you."

"Why has he killed so many wolves?"

"They prey on his people and his livestock. He pays a good bounty on them, and he has killed many by his own hand. These hides display his power over man and beast."

"He holds no power over me."

"No one in Christendom has power over you, Wulfhedinn."

I lowered him to the ground. "I will have my say with this king," I said.

"You shall. You shall," he said straightening his habit. "He will have much to say to you as well."

# Bastards Could Fare Worse

---

Brother Pyttel hitched up his hem and climbed a stack of crates piled high against the tent wall. He moved more lithely than I expected to the top. There, several strands of light filtered through small holes in the tent wall. He peered through one then gestured for me to follow.

"Come. You can see the assembly from here."

I climbed up and peeked through another hole.

*An image of many colors…*
*Lord Jesus Christ hangs from the cross*

My heart skipped a beat, and I pulled away. What was this vision? Had God come to me? I looked again.

*A Roman soldier stands below the Cross*
*Stabbing a spear between Jesus' ribs*

*The Holy Spear*
*Blood runs*
*From His crown of thorns, from impaled palms*
*From the scourging on his back*

*…running down my back*
*Pouring down shredded flesh*
*Hanging like red ribbons*
*Marked, scarred*
*Branded*

I waited to see it. I needed to see it, Jesus rising from the dead, but nothing moved. Nothing changed. He remained in agony, his face contorted under the crown of thorns.

*Cold corpse hanging*

I waited.

*The Raven alights on the crossbar*
*Above His shoulder*
*Ready to feed*

I lunged away from the peephole, my heart pounding. There was no grace, nor mercy, nor blessing where the Raven perches. I felt the cross around my neck and touched each of the saint's relics—ears, noses, bones. They were dead too, rotten and useless, as Pyttel had said.

*Knives peel hide, searing flesh*
*The anguish piled all around me*
*Within me*

*The Raven hungers*
*Return to the wilds, Wulfhedinn*

I scrambled down the crates and headed for the door.

"Where are you going?" asked Brother Pyttel.

"Away from here," I said.

He shook his head. "Defeated already? Did you not see the spear?"

"You do not want to know what I see...what follows me."

"We are all followed by something. No one is beyond redemption—even you." He smirked. "...or me."

I stopped.

"What did you expect?" he asked. "To be welcomed by angels? Have some patience, Gerwulf. Show some real faith." He gestured for me to return to his side. "You will find what you seek here, I promise."

I relented and climbed up again.

"I knew you would not give up so easily." He smiled. "Now, look again. You will see the Holy Spear and the tapestry of the crucifixion. It is truly inspirational—a masterpiece."

I returned to the peephole and found that the hellish nightmare was gone, replaced by a heavenly vision.

*Jesus raises his head*
*Calm face, touched by grace*
*Lit with promise...*
*Through the agony*
*There is salvation*

I had no words, just a feeling of warmth. It spread throughout me, making me sweat under the wolf skin.

The entire assembly now unfolded below me. There were

hundreds, more than I had ever seen gathered together peacefully. Beneath the tapestry, King Karl sat on his throne, presiding over his subjects like a lion, ready to spring. A king of men and beasts—but not of me.

He held a crude spear, gripping it with a thick, strong hand. The spearhead was pitted with rust, and the tip and edges were worn. The shaft was made of rough wood, yet it stood grander in the King's hand than a jeweled ceremonial weapon. It cast a glow across the crowd that had come to pay homage.

*The Holy Spear*
*Its light streaming through the tiny hole*
*A trace of God*
*Bathes my face in radiance*
*Soak it up, sense Him*
*...I kneel*
*And the light fades*

I shivered, the saint's bones rattling around my neck. "I must get closer to it," I said.

"You will, soon enough, after the assembly."

I mustered my patience and looked again, studying the King upon his throne. He wore a golden crown encrusted with gems that sparkled in the torchlight. A bright blue mantle spanned his broad shoulders, and a sword with a jeweled hilt hung at his side. His drooping mustache and golden red hair were trimmed neatly, his mane falling to his shoulders. His grooming set him apart from the long-haired, bearded Saxons, the wild pagans, he sought to rule.

Exotic striped furs covered the dais under his throne. Huge birds with sapphire plumage strutted freely across it. I had heard about such birds—peacocks. They wore their feathers as boldly as the King wore his great blue mantle. He scanned the crowd, searching for dissent and challenging every man there. No one looked him in the eye.

A large open fire burned in the center of the vast tent. Smoke vented through a hole in the high ceiling, supported by huge marble columns. Such columns belonged in a palace—not the pagan wilds. This king was displaying his wealth—and his power. With his garrison, Holy Spear, and mounds of dead wolves, he evoked an earthly power beyond anything I had seen. Could I fight for such a man?

> *I see myself*
> *Standing amongst the king's subjects*
> *As one of them*
> *…together*
> *Immersed in the light of the Holy Spear*
>
> *I approach the king, high upon his throne*
> *…abandon the wolf pelt*
> *Stripped to fresh pink skin, my back whole*
> *Kneeling*
> *…bathing in the light of the Holy Spear*
> *Delivered*

The image vanished as rapidly as it appeared. I blinked hard, trying to bring it back but could only see the King and his assembly. I needed to learn more about him and those who surrounded him.

His seven children stood to his left, his queen to his right. She held her head proudly, a flawless face, like that of a saint. Mother, lover, queen; I could fight for such a woman.

The King had four sons and three daughters. A nursemaid

cradled an infant, and several toddlers fidgeted next to her. They quieted when their father scowled at them.

The oldest child was a youth of about thirteen, a gangly boy with a crooked back, a hunchback. He loomed over the younger children. His face was different too, unlike the beautiful queen's features.

"Who is the boy with the hooked back?" I asked.

"The King's eldest, Pepin the Hunchback," said Brother Pyttel. "His mother was the King's first wife. Many call her a concubine and Pepin a bastard because the marriage was made by old Germanic custom. The bishops denounced it, so the King set her aside, and properly married Hildigard, his queen now. Some say he did it for love, some say for politics." The monk chuckled. "Despite this, the King accepts Pepin, his first-born, as legitimate, and treasures him, as he does all his children, including his bastards."

On a lower dais were several other beautiful women. They were richly dressed and surrounded by more children, who all bore a resemblance to the King. Royal concubines and their bastards.

"Bastards could fare worse," I said.

"Indeed."

# An Old Myth

---

The assembly lasted long into the night. There were so many in the crowd that I could not focus on them all at once, so I narrowed my sights. Several bishops stood behind the King. They wore mitered headdresses and held long staffs shaped like shepherds' crooks, but topped in gold instead of wood. The one with the biggest staff chewed his lips as he gazed at the Holy Cross.

Two large shaggy wolfhounds sat at the King's feet. Their noses turned in my direction behind the tent wall. They smelled me, jumped up, and barked until the King snapped his fingers. They lowered their heads and settled back at his feet, keeping their ears alert.

Frankish nobles and foreign emissaries stood closest to the dais. The Saxon chieftains with their round faces, along with the rest of the crowd, were relegated behind the Franks. The Saxons had cropped their hair and beards roughly, trying to imitate the civilized Frankish style. It made them look all-the-more heathen.

I searched the faces of the Saxons, looking for the one who had raped my mother. I would know him if I saw him, like me—with the wolf demon in his eyes. It was unlikely that he would be here, paying homage to King Karl, but I stared at each of them until sure of it.

The King pounded the spear three times. "Present the Saxon chieftains," he said.

Several dozen Saxons approached the King, carrying tributes of swords, golden broaches, embroidered textiles, and silver. Each chieftain was accompanied by a youth who was announced as his son. The first were the most richly dressed—likely the leaders of the strongest clans.

King Karl scanned them and interrupted the presentation. "Hessi, where is Widukind, chieftain of the Westphalian Saxons?"

One of the Saxons stepped forward. He wore a mantle clasped with a golden broach that was larger than the King's. He bowed, rubbing his hand across a large nose and thin lips. "He has failed to come, My King."

"Why does he refuse to obey his King's summons to assembly?" he asked impatiently.

"We have heard many things. He may be hiding in the north where his brother-in-law, King Sigfred of the Danes, offers him protection. Others say that he has returned to Saxony."

"Why is he not *here*—at *my* assembly?" the King snapped. "Where is Sidag?"

A Saxon with a calm, open face approached the dais and bowed.

"Sidag, cousin of Widukind," said the King. "What do you

know of his whereabouts?"

He bowed deeply. "My King. There are many rumors…"

"Rumors of wolf warriors?" asked the King. "I have heard these too. What truth to them?"

Sidag hesitated, keeping his head down. "Merely peasant gossip, Sire."

Hessi stepped in. "There is too much talk to be idle gossip. I believe that Widukind and his followers are reviving the ancient pagan rites, invoking the Devil to become Wulfhednar."

"How many?" the King asked.

"Maybe a dozen elite warriors from the ranks of the nobility, his inner circle," said Hessi.

"But the King's massive Christian army can certainly defeat a dozen heathen warriors," said Sidag, lifting his head. "Even if they are the best in Saxony."

"The best in Saxony should be in *my* army," The King roared, pounding the Holy Spear on the dais.

"Sire, Widukind is gathering even more support," said Hessi. "Every day free and half-free farmers join him from all over Saxony." He pointed a bony finger at Sidag. "I hear that many of them are Sidag's own peasants."

The crowd murmured.

"I have tried to help my cousin and my people to see reason," said Sidag, "to accept your rule, to embrace baptism and peace for the good of all our people who have suffered in these endless wars…"

Hessi snorted. "Sidag, you turn a blind eye when your people crawl back into the forest to sacrifice to Wodan and call upon the pagan demons!"

"And what of *your* peasants?" Sidag asked. "Are they so well in hand? They also stray from Christ to follow the old ways."

Hessi lowered his eyes. "I assure you, Sire, that the Eastphalian Saxons under my authority are keeping the Christian faith and their loyalty to you," he said. "There is more that Sidag does not say. The heathen Danish king provides more than refuge for Widukind. We hear that he may offer the rebels military support."

The King jumped to his feet. "Where is the emissary from King Sigfred? I want them in front of me now!"

Five men with full barbarian beards approached King Karl carrying crates and baskets.

The first man bent a knee. "I am Halfdan, Ambassador of King Sigfred," he said with a thick accent. "King Karl, we bear gifts of friendship from King Sigfred. It is his desire to establish an alliance with the Great King of the Franks. We offer fine Danish trade and luxury goods."

"Lies!" said Hessi, flourishing his mantle like one of the King's peacocks. "It is commonly known that your king is bound by marriage to Widukind's sister and offers him refuge and support."

"Hessi, you too are bound to Widukind by marriage to his other sister," said Halfdan. "Perhaps he is hiding with you."

Hessi's face pinched, and he reached for his sword, but his belt was empty. None of the Saxons carried weapons. The King must have had them disarmed before entering the general assembly.

"I have been baptized and proven myself loyal to King Karl and God for many years," said Hessi. "You northern heathens, servants of the devil, are the deceivers."

Halfdan addressed the King. "King Sigfred is most sincere in his desire to make amends for the past," he said. "He seeks to establish diplomatic relations with the Great King Karl."

The King pondered this for a moment and said, "Present your gifts, Northmen."

They opened their baskets and crates and displayed furs, amber, honey, leather, swords, and a small coffer of silver coins. One of the King's magnates stepped forward to examine the goods. He stuck his long pointy nose close to the gifts then turned it up.

"That is Chamberlain Adalgis," Brother Pyttel whispered. "Responsible for the King's treasury and one of the most powerful of his military commanders, but I do not trust him."

"No one who is that close to a king's treasury can be trusted," I said.

"And he hates the heathens more than anyone else."

The Chamberlain poured out the honey and tossed aside the furs and leather, but paid particular attention to the weapons and silver coins. He swung the swords, checked their balance, and sneered. "Horse Master Gallo, what do you think of these Danish swords?"

A stout man climbed the steps, rocking from side to side on bowed legs. Several front teeth were missing, and his nose was as crooked as Pyttel's.

"The Royal Horse Master can break and train a mount better than anyone west of Constantinople," said Pyttel.

"He walks like an old man," I said.

"He had been thrown and kicked in the face by hooves more than anyone I know, but he rides like the wind."

Gallo inspected the Danish swords and scoffed. "Unfit for my Scola riders."

Adalgis lifted the coffer, estimating the silver's weight, and bit into several coins. "Is this all your heathen king offers?"

"This is but a small sample," the Ambassador said. "Our

wagons are loaded with large stores of these goods, as well as wheat, wool, iron, and dried fish. We also present the mighty King Karl with a special gift to honor his status as King of Beasts."

The Danes uncovered a large basket, and a litter of puppies scrambled out, tumbling and yelping. The wolfhounds studied them but did not move. A fluffy white pup with a black paw bounded to the King and jumped into his lap. It nipped at his arms and licked his face. He smiled, and the pup settled into his lap.

"They are special," said the Ambassador. "They are wolf pups, caught in the Danish wilds."

"Remove these beasts from the court!" Chamberlain Adalgis ordered. "The only wolves that should be presented to the King are those that have been skinned."

"I must agree My King," said the bishop with the large staff, and the others nodded in agreement.

The Chamberlain grabbed several pups by the scruff and stuffed them back into the basket. They squealed and jumped out of the basket as soon as he turned his back. Several bit at his heels and latched onto the hem of his tunic, shaking their heads as if attacking prey. He swatted them, but they hung on stubbornly. The white pup stood in the King's lap and tried to howl. The Queen and several members of the court stifled grins, and the King's children giggled.

"If anyone can tame these beasts, you can, Great King of the Franks." The Danish Ambassador measured his words deftly.

Everyone waited for the King's response—except one of his daughters, a girl of about three years. She pulled away from her older sister and ran to the wolves.

"Puppies!" she screamed.

The King grinned. "Pick one for yourself, little Bertha." He gestured to his other children, including the bastards. "The rest of you, too." They ran to the pups, laughing.

Halfdan's lips curled subtly. He straightened his back and cleared his throat. "King Sigfred also wants to negotiate a truce between you and our Saxon relations. He asks that you stop your attacks on Saxony."

King Karl's smile vanished and his face flushed. "Sigfred can make no demands of me!"

At the sound of their father's angry voice, the children dashed back to their places, each carrying a squirming wolf pup.

"Saxony is part of the Frankish Kingdom, *my* kingdom," the King said. "There will be no attacks on the Saxons as long as they remain good Christian subjects and reject the rebel Widukind. Tell King Sigfred that I will reward him for turning over Widukind, but I will send my entire army to flay him alive if he continues to support the Saxon rebel." He held the pup up high by the scruff. It yowled, its feet kicking in the air. "I will conquer your wolves, your gods, and your king! Is that a negotiation you can understand?"

I thought he might kill the pup.

"It is quite clear," said Halfdan, setting his jaw. The Danes bowed, backed away from the dais, and disappeared into the crowd.

The bishops and many of the Frankish court tightened their lips with smugness. Hessi and the other Saxons shifted, their feet restless.

Karl sat and lowered the pup gently into his lap. "That is the only kind of diplomacy barbarians recognize. Now, the Saxons will swear their oaths."

Sidag approached the dais with a youth of about fifteen.

"My King, I present my son, Alric." They knelt and lowered their heads. "I, Sidag, make it known that I am a liege man of Karl the Great, King of the Franks. I will respond to the King's summons, aid the King in my own person, and send those warriors whose service I owe for the lands I hold." His words sounded rehearsed and empty. "I will do nothing to endanger the King, his family, his loyal nobles, or his royal power. I will stay true to my baptism and keep faith with the Lord, Our God, and not revert back to the worship of the devil and his demons."

His son repeated the oath, sounding no more earnest than his father.

Hessi and the rest of the Saxon chieftains approached the King with their sons and took their oaths. Some of the nobles had yet to be baptized, but they also promised to accept Jesus Christ and attend a baptism tomorrow at the Lippe River.

The Saxons' youths left their fathers' sides, but one boy, about seven years of age, clung to his father's leg. He glared at the child and nudged him. The boy hesitated then lowered his head and joined the others. The father's face clouded, his eyes glassy.

"Hostages?" I asked.

"The King requires each Saxon noble to give a son or closest male relative for fostering," said Brother Pyttel. "He gives the boys a place at court and educates them. He rewards their loyalty well, but his punishment is severe if their fathers rebel."

"Hostages," I repeated.

The King looked the boys over. "Strapping lads, fit to train and fight in the name of God," he said. "In exchange, I hereby grant the Saxon chieftains certain lands and titles. Saxony will be divided into counties, and each of you will be made a noble Count over your lands. You will act in my name under the jurisdiction of my army. You will enforce the law, administer justice, and ensure the building of churches and the baptism of your people. The new religious order will be overseen by my bishops and priests, advised by Alcuin of York, my scholar and court educator."

A man on the side of the dais bowed. His tunic was rough and undyed, like a monk's.

"That is my master, Alcuin," said Brother Pyttel. "He disagrees with some of the King's decisions in handling the Saxons. I daresay, he believes that Karl's insults and threats to the Danes were unwise."

"Do you side with your master or your King?"

"Both. King Karl does not mince words, and he has the personal and political might to carry out his threats. He also has God on his side, but Alcuin is a wise advisor. God directs Alcuin to influence the King in accordance with His plan. Of course, The Lord talks to me directly and listens to my replies, so the King always wants to know about it."

"I am sure," I said shaking my head.

The assembly continued. Several Frankish nobles approached the dais, each leading a young girl by the hand. The pairs were announced as noble Frankish fathers and their daughters, then each girl was presented to a Saxon Count for betrothal.

All but one of the girls appeared ready for childbearing. The youngest was only about nine or ten years old. She bit her lip and lifted her chin when she was presented to Count Hessi. He leered and nodded toward the King.

The bishop with the largest staff came forward. "Be it known that these Saxon Counts are betrothed to these women of Frankish noble lineage to create kinship and solidify alliances," he said. "In holy marriage and through the begetting of children, they unite two peoples into one Christian community under God. Lord, bless these unions and allow them to prosper for Your Glory, in the name of Jesus Christ."

"Amen," the crowd responded.

Brother Pyttel sighed. "He only gives them the younger daughters of his lesser nobles—not the cream of his kingdom. His generals would not marry their daughters to heathens. His top general, Theoderic, stands there, just behind the King. He is the King's cousin and his closest confidant."

General Theoderic was no longer young, but he stood tall and strong. He displayed several large scars on his bald scalp. His features were hardened, his gaze sharp and cunning.

"His words are few," said Pyttel, "but when he does talk, people listen—especially the King. Adalgis and Gallo are quite jealous of his confidence with the King."

Brother Pyttel's master Alcuin stepped forward on the dais. He held up a large vellum document and began to read. "Be it known to all Saxons that on this day, the Great King Karl, King of the Franks and Lombards, declares a new capitulary." His voice wavered. "These royal edicts and laws replace the barbaric Saxon laws and customs and are hereby established as the *Capitulatio in partibus Saxoniae*."

He looked up from the document. The crowd had fallen silent. "Be it known that if any Saxon hereafter hides from baptism and remains a pagan, let him be punished by death."

The crowd gasped, some muttering with surprise, others whispering while the King observed the new Saxon Counts closely.

Alcuin resumed, announcing a long list of offences punishable by death. They included cremating the dead in the pagan fashion, burning a church, and sacrificing to the old gods. Other capital offenses included breaking faith with the King and conspiring with pagans against Christians.

Through the elaborate words, I heard the King's message plainly—become one of us or die.

The decree continued. The Saxons were forbidden to hold public meetings except those ordered and overseen by the King's agents. They were also commanded to bury their dead in church cemeteries instead of pagan mounds.

Alcuin paused for a deep breath then said, "May Eve, Hexennacht, is soon upon us, so let it be known that all Saxons will be required to attend mass that night to protect themselves from the witches and demons that still roam their lands. In addition, Saxon women found meeting together, dancing around fire, or practicing magic on May Eve will be executed immediately."

"The King will tolerate nothing on the Night of the Witches, because it is sacred to the pagans," said Pyttel. "I think he secretly fears it. Most Christians do."

Alcuin still held up the document, ready to read more, but he hesitated.

"Continue," the King said.

Alcuin swallowed deeply. "The churches of Christ that are being built in Saxony should have greater and more illustrious honor than the shrines of the pagan idols have had. To accomplish this, Saxony will be divided into eight dioceses, each supervised by a bishop. The Saxons will provide labor to support the new churches and their priests and administration." He took another deep breath. "All Saxons will also pay a tithe to the church. This includes a tenth of all crops, possessions, and wealth."

The Saxon Counts roared in protest—all except Hessi, whose face remained expressionless. Others in the crowd murmured amongst themselves.

The King silenced the crowd with one thump of the Holy Spear.

Brother Pyttel cringed and shook his head. "The King is too hasty. These barbarians have no notion of paying tithes and need time to adjust to Christian practices. I am afraid this decree will only provide Widukind more fuel for his rebellion."

Count Hessi plastered a thin smug smile on his face. "The Eastphalian Saxons under my jurisdiction will comply," he said.

"That will be much easier for you than for me," said Sidag. "Your lands are far away, and your people have not suffered the devastation of the border wars as we have. Many of my people wander the wilds, homeless. This tithe is a great burden on us." He bent a knee to the King. "Sire, for God's mercy, I plead for time to rebuild our villages and allow the land to heal and become fruitful again."

"This is the price of your nobility," said Karl. "I allow you to keep your lands and grant you title over them. In return, you swear allegiance, administer your estates, and ensure the peasants become good Christians and pay the tithe. You will also provide soldiers for war when summoned. I will hold your sons in trust that you will honor your oaths."

"But My King…"

Karl interrupted. "I understand, however, the burden this puts on those who have lost the most. In light of Widukind's refusal to appear at my summons, his lands and estates are forfeited. I bestow his properties to you, Count Sidag. You will manage them wisely so they become productive enough to feed your people and pay the tithe."

Sidag's mouth hung open. "Thank you, My King," he said with defeat in his voice.

The King looked to Hessi. "I am also charging the Saxon nobles—including you, Hessi—with bringing in the heretic Widukind," he said. "If you fail me in this, you will lose far more than lands and titles."

Sidag and Hessi glared at each other, their hatred clear.

"My King, we cannot find him if he wants to remain hidden," said Sidag.

Hessi stepped in. "One of the places he hides is the Externsteine, the sacred Raven's Stones, in the Teutoburg Forest."

Sidag frowned. "The peasants have spoken about the Raven's Stones for generations, but I have seen no proof of it myself. It is an old myth—nothing more."

"It is far more than myth," said Hessi. "It is said that the Externsteine is protected by Wulfhedinn warriors and the magic of a priestess—a witch. No Christian man can breach the powers she uses to shield them."

The crowd murmured. The King rubbed his chin, weighing all he had heard carefully. He raised his hand, and the crowd quieted. "I find there is often some small truth to rumors and myths," he said. "We know that the Teutoburg Forest is a refuge for bandits and rebels, so it is likely they are practicing pagan worship there. They must be routed out."

"But most of the forest is untracked and impassible," said Hessi. "It is impossible to lead a force of any size through there."

"I am well aware of that," said the King. "Before I can invade, the royal road, the Hellweg, must be extended through the forest. I am tasking you, Sidag, to clear a route that is wide enough for my army to march unimpeded."

"But, Sire," he said. "It would be safer and easier to widen the known travelling routes that skirt around the thickest parts of the forest."

"I will leave you a contingent of soldiers to protect the work. You will use your slaves and free and half-free peasants for labor."

"The free peasants will resist," Sidag said.

"*Make* them," the King commanded. "Take heads, peel flesh from bones if you must, but you will clear a road and rout out the rebel Widukind, his demon warriors, and his witch. This rebel *will* submit to me. He will bend a knee to God and accept baptism, then he will kiss my ass."

# What Manner of Beast

*The* general assembly concluded, and the King left the assembly hall escorted by his guard.

"Wait here," said Brother Pyttel. "I will talk to him."

I paced among the piles of wolf skins. I would not wait long, but he returned shortly with the King. His royal presence filled the room, and the Holy Spear glowed with power in his hand.

The wolfhounds escorted him, and the wolf puppy tagged along behind. The hounds growled at me then heeled at their master's command. The pup whined and tucked its nose between the King's legs.

"Leave us, Pyttel," he said.

The monk lowered his head and left. The King set down the Holy Spear, flung off his magnificent blue mantle, and removed his crown. He laid them down together—within my reach.

Could this be?

*The wolf howls*
*Take the spear*
*…run…*
*Take it all*

I leaned forward. He watched me with a gleam in his eye and a curl in his upper lip. He appeared no less powerful without the spear and his royal effects. He was daring me to take them.

*The luster fades*
*A plain mantel, a dull crown*
*…a crude old spear*
*No glow, no light*
*God bestows His power, glory, and grace upon this king*
*…and everything he touches*

I backed away, knowing that the spear would remain a rusty antique in my hands.

The King smirked and ran his fingers through his hair. "You are Wulfhedinn?" His voice rumbled.

"I am Gerwulf."

"I know about you. The bastard damned by his father's blood—half Frank, half Saxon Wulfhedinn. An anomaly."

I bristled, but before I could respond he said, "My son, Pepin the Hunchback, is also an anomaly. It makes him tougher and smarter than the others. Now remove the monk's cloak so I can judge for myself what manner of beast you are."

This was no order. It was another challenge. This time, I accepted and dropped the cloak.

He examined my axes and wolf skin. His eyes were as clear

and steady as a man half his age. At the same time, they conveyed the cunning and wisdom of an elder twice his years. He showed no fear of me.

He unbuckled his sword belt and flung off his silk tunic. His chest and shoulders were broad, and his muscles were thick and marked by scars.

"They say you track and kill as well as the demon that possesses you," he said. "Brother Pyttel tells me that you can behead a man with one chop, but do you have the cullions to face me without your wolf hide and weapons?"

I set down my axes but left the skin on my back. I refused to bare it to anyone.

"Remove it," he said.

"You will *not* add my skin to your trophy piles."

"Not if we stand together as warriors—under God." His gaze rested on the cross around my neck. "You are Christian?"

"Yes."

"I have heard that you were educated in a monastery but were excommunicated for calling upon the powers of the wolf demon."

"For being what God Himself made me," I retorted.

"Do you summon the beast of your own will?"

"I have done what I have done."

"Which is it then, Wulfhedinn? Has God made you thus, or do you invoke such powers?"

I felt attacked—but his only weapons were words. I only knew one way to fight back.

*My axes beckon—within reach*
*Hands aching for them*

*Don the wolf hood*
*Kill this Christian King*
*Take the Holy Spear*
*Escape into the forest*

*The Raven calls*
*Return to my realm*

Before I could grab my axes, I heard Pyttel's words, as if he were standing next to me, whispering in my ear.

*Submit to God*
*Submit to His king*
*Fight for your soul*

It would be easier to run…

*Back to the forest*
*Every night unchanged*
*Alone with the Raven when darkness falls*
*The morning sun blinding me*
*Chasing me into the shadows*
*Another night, another day*
*Lost to the Raven*
*I could bear her no longer*

I left my weapons where they lay. I reached instead for my cross, preparing for a different kind of fight.

"Brother Pyttel tells me you know some measure of Latin," the King said. "Prove it."

"*Fallaces sunt rerum species.*" The language of holy men

flowed from my lips, unspoken since youth.

A smile passed under the King's long moustache. "Yes, the appearances of things are deceptive," he translated. "So you *are* the Wulfhedinn of which we hear, the boy from the monastery who forfeited his mortal soul for invoking the wolf spirit."

I locked my eyes on his. "Yes."

"What about the rest of your story?"

"There is no more to tell."

"One of the monks at your monastery was found dead in the forest, mutilated as if torn apart by wolves. Some say it was you."

"Some say it was wolves."

"Yes, perhaps, but I need to know why the bastard of a Saxon Wulfhedinn would risk sneaking into my camp to offer service to me."

"I am also a Frank—one of yours."

The King flinched. It was subtle, but I saw it.

"I could have you killed as you stand here before me," he said.

"Then do it."

He smoothed his moustache. "I think not. You have the heart of a beast and the keen mind of an educated man. I do not waste talent."

The King called Brother Pyttel back into the room. "Give him the mantle," he said.

Pyttel handed me a red mantle. It was made of heavy wool and lined with fox fur. Embroidered with black ravens on the edges, it was fine enough for a king—or a man who thought himself one.

"Can you find the man who wore this?" asked the King. "It belongs to Widukind, the leader of the Saxon rebellion. He has traded his nobleman's cloak for the skin of the wolf and has rallied a band of demon Wulfhednar against me. None of my Saxon nobles or my trackers has been able to locate him."

I smelled a distinct scent in the fabric—a mix of sweat from wielding heavy weapons, of blood, and of death. Only the strongest warriors could rival it.

"I have hunted more difficult prey," I said.

"Good," he said. "Track him and those who shelter him, especially the nobles. The Danish king has given him sanctuary in the North, but there are rumors that he is now hiding at the Externsteine near here in the Teutoburg Forest. Pagans believe the place is protected by the magic of a witch. Find his lair, learn how to breach its defense, and report back to me in secret." He leaned close and whispered. "Invoke the Devil and every demon in Hell if you must—just *find* him." He furrowed his brow, and his eyes turned to stone. "I would conspire with Satan himself to have Widukind cowering at my feet with his tail between his legs. He must be humbled before God—in front of my entire kingdom."

"And if I do this, what will you do for me?" I asked.

"I will ensure you are restored to the Church, as long as you repent of your sins. If you are successful in this, the rewards will be great, both here and in heaven—for both of us."

He had laid it before me, the promise of a king, the one who holds the Holy Spear and makes it come alive. God's King. I could almost taste the redemption he offered.

*Fight for your soul*
*You can recover it here*

The King picked up the Holy Spear and aimed it at my throat. "If you betray me…" He raised his voice and turned to launch the spear into a pile of wolf skins. "…I will hunt you down and skin you alive. Do we understand each other?"

"Clearly."

The monk's face lit up, and he made the sign of the cross. "For the glory of God! To bring the last of the heathen into His Kingdom."

"Into *my* kingdom," the King said.

I dropped Widukind's red cloak and claimed my weapons.

Brother Pyttel picked it up. "You will need the rebel's mantle to track him."

"I never forget a scent." I headed for the door, Brother Pyttel at my heels.

"Gerwulf," the King called after me. "Remove those rotten pieces of flesh from your neck, but never, ever lose your cross."

# Suffer the Darkness

*Throngs* of people swarmed the alleyways between tents after the King's general assembly. Brother Pyttel and I blended unnoticed into the crowd and overheard much talk. The voices of nobles mixed with those of free peasant farmers. They debated the major events of the meeting, especially the King's new laws for Saxons. Tension was as thick as campfire smoke.

"The King's new taxes and laws will drive those Saxon savages into outright rebellion."

"He will break my back with these constant campaigns. I have fields to plant and livestock to tend."

"I do not have the resources of the aristocrats to be both a landowner and a soldier."

We heard many more complaints before slipping behind the wood pile and out the escape hole.

"Now you understand why bringing the rebel leader to

Christianity is so vital," said Brother Pyttel, setting the loose timber back in place. "If Widukind submits, I have faith that all the Saxon rebels will yield peacefully and accept God and the King's rule. It will save many lives and benefit all our souls."

"And the King's treasury," I muttered.

"Assuredly," he said. "It takes much silver to build the churches needed to bring the word of God to the heathen. It also takes a king of undeniable might to build a kingdom of one faith in God."

I smirked—death threats disguised as laws. I pictured the scars on King Karl's body and imagined the wounds he had inflicted on others. I had seen his great assembly tent, the masses cowering at his feet, the piles of wolf hides. He craved power— God's power—and God had given it to him.

"It is all for a greater good, I tell you!" Pyttel said as if reading my thoughts. "It is why God has given him the Holy Spear—to build His Kingdom on earth. We all must fight for it, me, you…the King. God has told me this."

"Assuredly." I said, seeing that I was not unlike most of them—only wanting what would help me. Even Pyttel was only trying to save his own soul.

"If you track down the rebel for the King, I have faith that you will attain what you seek," Pyttel said. "Now, how will you proceed?"

I returned his cloak and pulled the wolf snout over my face. "You do not want to know, brother."

"Yes, of course," he said. "When you return, seek me out, and I will take you safely to the King." He put his hand on my shoulder. "Be cautious. Most Saxons dare not tread far into the Teutoburg Forest at night. You can handle the thieves and bandits, but there are many evils there. I have felt the hot breath of demons on my neck in those woods."

"I *am* one of those demons," I said.

He smiled. "For now."

I ducked silently into the trees, hovered low, and disappeared. The misty air cooled my bare skin, so refreshing after the stuffy smoke-filled air of the King's camp. For a moment, I was almost glad to return to the forest, the place where I had hidden for so long. Yes, the King had promised me so much more, but his world was strange—and far less certain.

"Take care, and God be with you," Brother Pyttel called after me.

"God does not follow here," I muttered.

It was late, and I was tired, so I decided to wait until the following night to set out. I drew the wolf skin around me and bedded down. The skin was as much my own as anything, and there was comfort in that which I knew.

The next night, the forest beckoned, and I was free from guards and soldiers and kings.

*Nightfall shrouding me*
*The wolf bounds*
*…faster and faster…*
*Legs that never tire*
*…faster and faster…*

*The Raven soars down*
*keeping pace*
*Stay with me, Wulfhedinn.*
*I hunger*

*Feed the wolf*
*Feed the Raven*

The saints' bones tapped gently on my chest as I ran, forgetting the King's order to remove them. Within a mile, I picked up Widukind's scent. It was fresh; he had passed this way within the last day. If he had sought refuge far to the north with the Danes, he had returned now. He had probably lurked around the walls of the garrison and may have found a way inside, under the King's nose.

Before I could track him far, a sound stopped me. It was muffled—the sobbing of a girl. A high-pitched scream echoed through the trees…and another. The screaming stopped, and then a man shouted and grunted…another scream.

*Gut writhing, burning with fire*
*Mouth waters*
*Chest pounds*
*Sickened into fury*
*I want to kill…I need to kill…*
*I want blood*

I turned and bounded toward the noise. It took me a mile out of my way and down a narrow ravine. At the bottom, I found a soldier laying atop a girl half his size. He rammed her hard, punched her bloodied face, and rammed into her again.

*Know no mercy*

I flung my francisca, and it sunk in the back of his thigh. He screamed and rolled off. The girl curled into a ball, shivering, her naked body covered with blood and bruises.

I growled and jumped at him. My long axe swung around and around, over my head. His eyes darted, following the spinning blade. He tried to scoot away, but I sank it into his arm, slicing through flesh and bone. He wailed. I swung again.

*His blood tastes so sweet*
*The wolf rages, calling the Raven*
*Savor his fear*
*…revel in it*

He screamed and tried to move, but his life was draining from him. I aimed at his neck then thought better of it.

*No reprieve*
*Know how it feels*
*…buried in sin*
*Fiend, violator*
*Suffer the darkness*
*Join me…*

I lowered my sights and split his cullions. He shrieked, writhing, grasping weakly at his crotch with his remaining arm. I hacked, again and again, grunting and chopping, showering myself in his blood. When his face and body were unrecognizable, I took the head.

I bathed in the warmth of his blood until it cooled and dried on my skin. It marked me, but this time, I did not care. I could live with this stain.

*Raven*
*Beak open, ready to feast*
*She gorges*
*…quenched…never satisfied*

*Take him to Hell*

*Red eyes fade into blackness*
*Vanishing with the soul she carries*

*Bring me more, Wulfhedinn*

*Feed the wolf*
*Feed the Raven*

The girl trembled. Her face was swollen with purple bruises, and blood dripped from her nose and split lip.

"Go," I grunted.

Her bloody lip quivered. "What *are* you?" She sobbed, her eyes wide with fear. "Do not kill me!"

I pushed the wolf hood off my face and backed away. "Go! Now!"

She stood slowly, wrapping her arms around herself. She was older than I thought, old enough for marriage. I glanced at her naked body and back at her face. She may have been beautiful once—before today.

I tore the bloodied mantle off the soldier and tossed it to her. It dropped at her feet, but she hesitated to pick it up.

"Take it," I said.

Shaking, she wrapped it around herself and limped up the ravine. She glanced once over her shoulder and disappeared into the forest.

Her face lingered. Who was she, Saxon or Frank? Peasant, slave, or noble? I wondered what would become of her. Would she bear a bastard?

*She becomes another...*
*...the face of Mother*
*Battered and tainted*

*The Raven shrieks*
*Bring me more, Wulfhedinn*

I knelt and cleaned my axes on the grass, licking my lips, savoring the taste of his blood.

*The wolf craves it*
*Jaws ache for more*

*Feed the wolf*
*Feed the Raven*

*Then every night will remain unchanged*
*Alone with her when darkness falls*
*The morning sun blinding me*
*Chasing me into the shadows*
*Another night, another day*
*Lost to the Raven*

But he was deserving of this!

*Yet the Raven screeches*
*Haunts me*
*I could bear her no longer*
*It must end soon*

I reached for my cross, feeling the dried ears and fingers of the saints. I tore off the necklace, pulled off the relics one-by-one, then retied the cross around my neck.

# The Curse Poll

I climbed out of the ravine and picked up Widukind's scent. It led me toward Wodan's Spring—not far. I stopped. He was close, so easy to track, yet...

That place, that time...my stomach churned.

*Push it away, far under*
*...the place...the time*
*Long ago...gone now*
*Blackness...*
*All gone now*

I took a deep breath and a few steps toward the spring. A breeze rose, waking spirits in the rustling trees. I moved forward slowly, hoping Widukind's trail would take me in a different direction, knowing it would lead me to the spring.

*Soft light filters through the budding tree branches*
*Radiant blue funnel, flowing with sacred waters*
*It reflects everything*
*Sees everything*
*Eye of Wodan*

I almost turned around.

*Push it away, far under*
*…the place…the time*
*Long ago…gone now*
*Blackness…*
*All gone now*

The air smelled of rotting horseflesh. Had the rebel's mount died? The stink grew stronger as I approached the edge of the spring. I avoided looking at the Eye and caught sight of a horse, standing on the other side of the spring. Its hide was withered, its body gaunt. I moved closer, drawn to it.

It was dead, the head spiked on a pole, its eyes hollow. The hide hung behind, the legs dangling just above the ground.

A nithing pole, a curse pole, ancient pagan magic.

Widukind's potent scent filled the area, and there was another too, as powerful as his.

*Sweet musk and flowers*
*Spring flowers…*
*Tiny, delicate white blooms in a thorny thicket*
*Hawthorn*

*A woman*

*He rides with a woman*
*…and she is strong*

They had set the nithing horse so that it faced King Karl's general assembly. I approached and saw runes carved into the pole, some of them familiar.

*Wodan*
*Destruction*
*Dead man*

This was a cursed place for the King, for me.

The wind picked up and blew the horse's legs so they appeared to walk on air, its hooves skimming the ground.

*Blowing faster and faster*
*Until the nithing horse gallops*
*Pounding, shaking the ground*
*Across the waters and into the sky*
*Hooves thundering…*

*A herd stampedes from above*
*A shriek echoes through the forest*
*Like ice on my neck*
*Like death on my shoulder*

*Mighty warrior, spear in hand*
*Raven's head and woman's breasts*
*Riders follow across the sky*
*Bones with no flesh…dead riders on dead horses*

*The wind rises*
*Blowing faster and faster*
*...carrying the scent of sweet musk and hawthorn...*
*The shield maiden, tall atop her black mount*
*Black wings stretch in flight*

*Ride with us, Wulfhedinn*

*They sweep down and charge*
*Fiery hooves brush past...*
*Climbing into the sky*

*...and the Raven soars above...*

The nithing horse remained, staked on its pole, swaying silently in the wind.

*The taste of blood lingering...*

I wiped my mouth, but my hand remained clean.

*You will not take me*
*Fight for your soul*

I tore the horse from the pole and hacked it until the head was smashed, and the hide was shredded. The spirits would exact a price for destroying it, but the power of the Christian King and his promise of redemption emboldened me. My act would anger the man who erected it more than the spirits—and I was afraid of no man.

I left it in the muddy bank and found two sets of tracks,

made by large war horses. They led to a narrow animal trail that ran along a streambed. I followed it for a couple of miles to a clearing of untilled fields, overrun with sprouting weeds.

The fallow land surrounded a burned-out Saxon village. There was little remaining of the village but a few charred walls—the ruins of one of the King's Saxon campaigns. It appeared abandoned, but I was not alone.

*Ghosts linger here*
*Sparks soaring into the sky*
*Landing on my face…*
*She lies battered and tainted*
*…then floats*
*Like ashes blown in the wind*

*The face of a woman*
*…the face of Mother*

*Push it away, far under*
*…the place…the time*
*Long ago…gone now*
*All gone now*

*The Raven perches on a charred cross*
*Fallen from the church*
*Fat and glossy*
*Preening her plumage*
*…quenched…never satisfied*

My hands began to tremble, and I ran.

# Good Subjects
of the King

Widukind's scent and that of the woman led away from
the village. Their horse tracks were easy to see in the dirt.
They rode an overgrown path that gradually grew wider and
well-worn, becoming a road of sorts. Soon, human footprints
and the tracks of their dogs and pigs littered the well-trodden
route. I ducked off and followed it from the cover of the forest.
It ran to the edge of more farm fields and another village.

These fields were planted and bursting with tender green
shoots. Cooking smoke emerged from under the eaves of the
cottages. Wattle fences enclosed tilled gardens and livestock
pens that smelled of fresh dung. This village was alive.

Chatter and laughter came from inside the homes. Fire-
light flickered through gaps under doors, likely barred for the
night. In the center of the village was a small church, a wooden
cross rising above the roof.

I trotted through a field, hopped the fence, and headed

for the largest building, probably the hall of the village elder. Someone opened the door and threw out a handful of bones. Several dogs snarled and snapped, competing for the scrap. I circled downwind and snuck up to a shuttered window. Voices emerged through a large crack.

Women chattered, and their children teased each other with high pitched squeals. I focused on the deeper voices speaking in hushed tones, a group of about two dozen men. I glimpsed two of them through the crack. One was young without a beard. The other had streaks of grey in his full beard.

"Our nobles reap more lands and titles by licking the boots of the Frankish king and his god," the young one complained bitterly.

The older man nodded. "They grow richer and can afford to pay his outrageous new tithe, but it will break my back."

There were murmurs of agreement from the other men in the hall.

"They will pinch us out so that we have to sell our freedom to them to pay our debts!"

Here was proof that Widukind had spied on the King's assembly and had moved rapidly through Westphalia ahead of me. He was spreading the word about the King's new tithe—and dissension amongst the lower Saxon classes. I tilted my head, trying to hear more through the shutter.

Another voice piped in. "Soon the King will also demand that we fight in his campaigns. How am I supposed to sow crops and fight wars too?"

The others grumbled in agreement, and the conversation heated up. "It is bad enough we have had to accept his God. Now we will be slaughtered for worshiping our own gods, for following the ways of our ancestors—*our* ways!"

"...and he plans to extend his royal road so he can march his army straight through the forest and trample our lands at his will!"

"...not as long as I can hold a spear in my hand!"

They pounded their drinking mugs against the table and roared in agreement.

"We must wait for what fortune the nithing pole brings—and for Widukind's call." This voice was steady and decisive, likely that of the village elder.

Footsteps approached the window, and someone unlatched it. I ducked into the shadows. A women opened the shutter, dumped the contents of a pot outside, and closed the shutter. A rancid smell filled the air. I returned to the window, stepping around the mess.

"Wodan will not favor us unless we prove that we have the courage to act as warriors," another man said. "I want my vengeance now!"

"We must act wisely," the elder replied. "We will prepare and wait until the time is right, as Widukind says. We have only been spared from the King's wrath because he believes us loyal to him and his God. For now, we must continue to act as such."

"I have waited long enough!" the young one said. "I despise their weak god and will not forgo our rites of May Eve to bow my head in church. Their god has no power over Wodan, and King Karl has no power over me! I would burn that church to the ground right now and kill every man the King sends after me. That would show Wodan my courage."

"You will obey me as long as I can best you with sword and spear—or my bare fists," said the elder. "We have seen how rashness worked in the neighboring village. They were butchered; their homes and fields destroyed while our own nobles—

some our blood kin—were rewarded for turning them over to the Franks."

"They died as warriors and are drinking with Wodan in the great hall of Walhalla now," said the elder's son, "...not attending mass and licking the balls of Christian priests!"

A brawny arm knocked the youth to the ground, spilling his beer.

"First you will lick mine, boy," the elder said, and the others laughed. "We may not have the wealth of the nobles, but we are free men. If we want to remain free, we must follow Widukind's wisdom and give him time to rally the clans from the north and east. When we join together, then Wodan will see our courage in battle."

The other men debated loudly amongst themselves until a woman's voice interrupted. "I lost my parents and two brothers and their families in the last Frankish raids," she said. "We all have family and friends that have been killed. We have all lost too much already. You are brave fighters, but the Elder is right. This village cannot defeat King Karl alone.

"Widukind has forfeited everything to fight for us, the free peasants, including his noble titles and lands. He is favored by Wodan and can summon the powers of the Wulfhedinn. With him, we can beat this king with his weakling god, but we must be patient and follow his plan."

The youth scoffed, but the rest pounded their drinking cups on the table in approval.

The elder raised his voice. "It is agreed. For now, we wait. We go to mass, sow the fields, and pretend to be good subjects of the King and of God. Soon enough, we will muster to Widukind's call. That is how it is and how it will be."

They toasted, and the conversation turned to discussions of

livestock and planting fields.

Moving away from the window, I pondered what I had heard. As Count Hessi had said, Widukind was gathering a large following amongst the peasants across large areas of Saxony.

And he was summoning Wulfhednar, a dozen warriors, maybe more.

I wondered for a moment if the Raven shadowed those wolf warriors too. I slipped out of the village and picked up the rebel's trail.

# Silvery Gods Rising

The tracks led northeast. Thick stands of evergreens blocked much of the moonlight, and when a cloud passed over the moon, the tracks disappeared. The woods grew thicker over several miles, swallowing the path, but the scent of Widukind and his woman companion was strong enough to follow. I crawled over a large fallen tree trunk. I began to feel uneasy, edgy—more so than I had in any other forest.

A branch rubbed against another, moaning like a dying animal. It startled me, and I tripped and fell. I lay there for a moment, stunned by my own clumsiness.

*Something creeps around my ankles*
*Slithers up my legs*
*...wrapping, squeezing...*
*Like snakes*
*...wrapping, squeezing...*

I reached immediately for my francisca.

*Creeping up…belly and chest*
*Pulling me, drawing me in*
*Crushing my breath*
*Gasping*

I swung wildly, hacking and chopping.

*One vine cut, two sprout up*
*Creeping up…neck and head*
*…wrapping, squeezing…*

I slashed madly.

*Cutting, slicing myself*
*Blood flying*

I broke free and clambered to my feet. Choking for breath, I stumbled through the dark, running toward a patch of light… a clearing where the moon shone. There, I stopped, panting, my heart pounding.

Catching my breath, I looked for the cuts and slashes I had inflicted on myself, but my flesh remained intact. I ran my hands over my body and head several times to be sure but felt nothing, not a scratch nor a single drop of blood.

There was strong magic in this forest—more powerful than that at Wodan's Spring—and it was set here to protect something.

The Externsteine, the Raven's Stones.

It must be nearby. I grasped my cross, surprised to find it hanging around my neck.

*You will not take me*
*I will not be deterred*

*Fight for your soul*

The scent of Widukind and the woman rider was strong here. I found their tracks and followed with both axes in hand. Their trail took me across the field and into another stand of trees. The woods were thinner here. Moonlight streamed through the branches, and I picked up my pace, drawing closer. The cover thinned, and a heavy smell of hawthorn blossoms filled the air. I trotted past hedges dripping with the white spring flowers.

*My head light*
*Spinning*
*Stirred by thick sweetness...*
*...a honeyed woman*
*A beautiful queen who conceives the heirs of a king*
*Proud upon the throne*
*Naked in his bed*
*Thick sweetness...*
*The taste of her flesh*

The hawthorn grew thicker, fencing the path on both sides until the thorny branches scratched and tore at my legs and wolf skin.

*The Raven flies*
*And the perfume fades*

I sniffed deeply to recapture the vision, but it was gone; stolen by her.

*Thorns piercing deeper*

I slashed at the brush to clear a path, wondering how they rode horses through the tangled mass. Somehow, they did, their scent leading me forward.

*The thorns sink deeper and deeper*
*Arms, legs, body, and head*
*Piercing my skull*
*With a crown of thorns*
*Forsaken by God...*

*She shrieks*
*Blood of the violated upon her beak*

*Naked and trembling*
*Beaten face, battered body*
*Torn and impaled...*

*Blood running down my back*
*Pouring down shredded flesh*
*Hanging like red ribbons*

*Blood splattered from the wolf's prey*
*More dead, more sins*
*The Raven growing fatter*

I ripped free of the thorns and ran through a small gap in the thicket. Again, my flesh was whole and dry. I grasped my cross, standing next to a stream, disoriented. How much time had passed? An hour or a hundred years? Everything was strange and unfamiliar, and all sense of direction was lost.

*You will not take me*
*I will not be deterred*

*Fight for your soul*

I caught Widukind's scent and followed. I trotted along the stream until the ground grew damp and thick moss muffled my steps. The trees opened, and my foot sank into mud. I tried to step back but stumbled and fell.

*The muck holds tight, pulling me down*
*…shackled to a great weight*
*Dragging me deeper*
*Legs, body, and arms*

I swung my axes, trying to sink them into something solid, slicing through nothing but air.

*Pulling deeper…*
*Neck and head*
*…choking…flailing*
*Entombed*
*…Choking…flailing*

My axe brushed something. I swung again and it lodged into a fallen tree trunk. I pulled myself along it until I reached dry ground and threw myself out of the mud, coughing and panting. After catching my breath, I saw that only one foot was muddy, and the rest of my body was clean and dry. I grasped my cross.

*You will not take me*
*I will not be deterred*

*Fight for your soul*

I stood slowly, and there they stood. Giant pillars of white stone towered above me in the moonlight, more than twenty times my height.

*Mist swirls*
*Veiling the giants*

I rubbed my eyes, trying to glimpse more, creeping forward, feeling for solid ground with every step.

*They re-emerge from the mist*
*…silvery gods rising out of the bog…*

*The Raven soars*
*You have come to my stones, Wulfhedinn*

*The fog rises again*
*Surrounding me*
*In foreboding chill*

*A wolf calls in the distance*
*Its cry answered by another, then another*
*…the call of a pack*
*Coming from all directions*
*Surrounded…*
*…signaling attack*

*The noise fades*

*Quiet…too still*

I turned several times, listening, trying to see through the fog. I turned again.

*A wolf jumps from the mist*
*Snapping, biting*
*…gone*

*Snarling from behind*
*Fangs bared, lips curling*
*Hungry breath in my face*

I swung at it.

*…gone*

*Another leaps, and another*
*Assault from every direction*

I wanted to kill every one of them. I struck out over and over until my arms ached and sweat ran down my body.

*They howl together again…*

I hit something solid. It cracked like wood—a wolf face carved into a tree trunk. I hacked at the face until it was splintered, and the tree threatened to topple. Glancing around, I saw many more. I was surrounded by wolves carved into trees—a pack of wooden wolves.

I grasped my cross.

*You will not take me*

The Raven's Stones had vanished, but the scent of Widukind and the woman was strong, leading me on. The rebel leader meant to lure me into another trap in the forest.

I would not be the fool twice.

I ran the opposite way. Soon the trees thinned and opened to a meadow. The moon and the stars came out. My head cleared, and I regained a sense of direction.

I turned and looked back the formidable palisade of bewitched woodland around the Raven's Stones. I had learned enough about its magical defenses and everything else the King had wanted to know: the whereabouts of Widukind and those who sheltered him, and the secret place where the Saxons worshiped the old gods.

I trotted southwest toward the King's camp. After a couple miles, I heard steps behind me. I stopped. Only my heartbeat broke the silence, so I moved on.

*Steps…steps…*
*…faster…closer*

I hastened my speed.

*Faster…closer…horse's hooves*
*Sweet musk teasing me*
*…mixing with hawthorn*
*Scent of the woman rider*

*Black figure in the trees*
*High atop a steed*
*Wielding shield and spear*
*Her mount snorts and stomps*

I picked up my pace and broke into a run.

*She gives chase*
*On my heels*
*Horse's breath hot on my neck*

I darted between trees, brush, and boulders then ducked under a tree that had fallen against another.

*The pounding of hooves fades*
*…and is gone*

I clenched my cross, gasping for breath.

*You will not take me*

# As One with Them

‹~~~›

The woman had given up the pursuit quickly. She likely still followed at a distance, waiting for a better opportunity to attack. I snaked through rough terrain and waded in a stream to cover my scent. After a mile of wet feet, the forest thinned. I left the stream and the branches opened to let me pass. I breathed a little easier and pushed hard through the night.

Dawn was breaking when I neared the King's camp. It seemed a new day, different than the others. Today, darkness would not pull me away from the light; I had news for the King, yet it was still too dangerous for me to sneak into camp alone. I considered waiting for night, but before I could ponder it further, the breeze carried the unmistakable stink of incense, stale beer, and goat's blood to me.

Brother Pyttel.

His scent was fresh from this morning. It led from the direction of the escape hole toward Wodan's Spring. I groaned.

What was this monk's obsession with bathing? And why did he have to bathe *there*? I decided to wait where I was for his return.

The sun rose higher in the sky, and I waited and waited... how long could it take to wash? Did he drown himself? I thought of the nithing horse and wondered if he had seen its remains on the bank of the spring.

Near midday, I could stand it no longer. I pulled up the hood, believing that the wolf would be safer than the man and walked to the spring.

*The blue glow appears*
*Visible in daylight*

I crept low and avoided looking at the Eye as I came to the edge of the spring.

*Push it away, far under*
*...the place...the time*
*Long ago...gone now*
*Blackness...*
*All gone now*

I scanned the area. The nithing horse was staked upright on the bank again. Its smashed head was whole, its shredded hide restored, legs swaying in the breeze. The scent of Widukind and the woman permeated the place as if mocking me.

I paused, stunned.

Who had been tracking whom?

They knew I had destroyed their curse upon King Karl. They let me follow them into the forest and led me into the hazards that protected Raven's Stones. They made me the fool...no one had ever succeeded in tracking *me* before.

Had they staked a new curse—or had they raised the one I had smashed with magic? Did it matter? I shivered.

*The spirits call to me*
*Horse's hoof*
*And black wing that rides its back*

*Return to the wild*

*Snarling, snapping*
*Raging in my ears*

*You will not take me*
*I will fight for my soul*
*And I will win*

Brother Pyttel was there, naked and laying prostrate under the horse. He mumbled to himself, his mouth grinding into the dirt as the horse swayed over his back. His muttering grew louder, becoming a rant that ended with a shout.

What was the madman doing now?

He picked up an urn, lifted it over his head, and tipped it. Blood spilled out, running down his face and over his naked body. He rubbed the blood and congealing clots over his body and smeared it onto his cock until it rose. He lifted his head and arms and said, "Wodan, I come to you naked, awakened, and covered in the blood of sacrifice in defiance of my own God. Accept my offering and know that your power is acknowledged by both pagan and Christian."

The crazy Christian monk was performing pagan sacrifice—a rite punishable by death.

He took a raw piece of meat from the basket—a goat's heart. He raised it over the Eye and said, "Mighty Wodan, god of wisdom, courage, and victory; I, a humble monk and priest of the new God, give thanks for all your blessings."

He waded into the spring and took a bite of the heart and placed it into the Eye. The water turned red, washing the blood from his body. "Mighty Wodan, father of Widukind, I beseech you. Become as one with my God, for the sake of your people and mine."

He was not the first Christian or the first monk I had seen in sacrilege. He was like some of the others, gratifying himself by answering temptation, lured by the power of the old gods and the old magic. Yet he was different, the soldier monk with the crooked face that shone with madness—a holy fool. He had not condemned me, and he freely confessed his own sin. Now, he had made himself vulnerable to me. I stepped from behind the brush in plain sight, ensuring that he knew I had seen everything.

He bounded out of the water and scooped up his discarded clothing. I turned toward camp, the monk chasing after.

"Gerwulf!" he called, his bare feet stumbling. "Stop! Come back!"

I began to run, making him stumble after me. When I had passed beyond the light of Wodan's Eye, I stopped. He soon appeared, a look of panic plastered on his blood-stained face.

"Gerwulf! Why are *you* here?"

"Why are you here?"

"You must tell no one," he pleaded. "It is not as it appears. I am faithful to my God and My King." He pulled out his cross and put it back around his neck. "Did you see? They have staked a nithing horse, a dire curse upon the King! I do what I must in the Eye of Wodan—a gesture of respect to him, performed *his* way to appease the old gods, to break the curse. This place, this spring, is holy! Its sanctity should flow from the old gods to the new. He has accepted me, which means his people will also accept me, and our God."

"You fool," I said. "Wodan does not accept you as a Christian. You are embracing *him* as a pagan. You are becoming one of them."

"No! I only seek to be *as one* with them. Only then can I reach their hearts to convert them to the One True God and save their souls."

"Do you think you have the strength to placate pagan spirits? You see what their demons have made of me. Is that what you want?"

He wiped his mouth then gazed at the blood on his hand. His trembling fingers reached for my wolf skin. He pulled away and felt his own scarred face, the color draining from his cheeks.

"Why have you returned so soon?" he snapped, fumbling to put his clothes back on.

"I have done everything the King wanted," I said.

"In one night? Impossible."

"You will take me to the King now, or I will surprise him in his bed as Wulfhedinn—and tell him what you were doing at the spring."

"You will tell him either way," he said.

I let him dwell on it.

He sighed. "Come then. The King will be in his tent."

On the way back to camp, I thought about what the monk had done at the spring. He was no longer a holy man in my eyes. He was simply Pyttel—and I liked him the better for it.

# Demon Magic and Intimidation

The King was breaking his fast in his private quarters, dressed in a simple linen tunic. His sword was sheathed and hanging on a peg, and the Holy Spear was within his reach, leaning against a tent post. He made no attempt to reach for either when we entered the tent.

"Sit, Wulfhedinn," he ordered. His dogs and the wolf pup lowered their heads and sat, but I remained standing. The King chuckled then scowled at Pyttel. "Leave us, monk."

Pyttel hesitated. "But My King..." he stammered.

"Leave."

As he left the room, Pyttel's brow twisted, pleading with me to keep his secret.

The King cut a piece of cheese and addressed me harshly. "You refuse a king who invites you to sit at his morning table?"

"I am here to give my report."

"So quickly?"

"I have learned everything you wanted to know."

"I expected no less." The King filled a cup with beer and pushed it across the table to me. "The rebel must be nearby."

I hesitated.

He furrowed his brow. "You think that your mangy presence merits wine?" he asked, filling his own cup. "I prefer good Frankish beer, and so will you."

I sat and drank. A rich malty aroma filled my nose. The beer ran creamy smooth over my tongue—like no beer I had tasted. I took a longer swig.

The King smeared a thick layer of butter on a hearty piece of bread. "If you have bad news, you are wise to come to me in the morning when I am in my best humor."

"You must come with me outside the camp."

He took a large bite of the bread. "I *must* do nothing."

"You must see it for yourself."

"See what?" He took a long gulp of beer. "If you intend to lure me away to kill me, you will be disappointed."

"If I wanted to kill you, you would be dead by now. I stand with you—as fellow Christians, under God."

He downed the last of the beer, belched and picked his teeth.

"It is very close to camp," I said, "and others will find it soon. It is so near that they will question your authority, your blessing from God when they see it."

His eyes flashed. "Yes, then. Take me there."

We took Pyttel and made our way through camp. The King had disguised himself in a ragged cloak, tucking his sword and the Holy Spear under it. I was covered by Pyttel's cloak again. It was torn and filthy…strange considering how often he bathed. We looked like three beggars stealing through the alleyways.

Once outside the wall, Pyttel could no longer contain himself. He was frantic. He picked at himself, as if removing fleas, and babbled nervously. "The spring…nothing there at the spring…nothing to tell…my killing time is over…it is over, I tell you!"

"Hell's blazes, Brother Pyttel! Shut up!" the King said then leaned toward me. "He is as deranged as a rabid bat. My bishops say it is punishment for his sins…but yet, he has a way with the heathens. They believe he is touched by the gods, and he converts more of them than any of my other missionaries."

"He does have a way," I said.

Pyttel quieted but continued to squirm, stealing desperate glances at me all the way to the spring.

It was easier this time to approach the Eye.

*You will not take me*
*I will fight for my soul*
*And I will win*

The nithing horse rode like a ghoul on its pole, casting its empty eyes on us. A gust of wind blew up, whipping dead leaves around it and making the legs sway.

King Karl's face flushed, and the vein in his forehead bulged. "Who dares stake a curse pole at my spring?" he demanded.

"Widukind," I said.

"You know this?"

"I tracked him. He was here, and he was likely in your camp at the general assembly, watching everything."

The King approached the nithing horse boldly, his face twisting with rage. "You were right to bring me here. I had to confront this offense, this *sacrilege*, myself."

"My King, stay away!" Pyttel said, making the sign of the cross. "We must leave this place now!" He dropped to his knees. "Nothing at the spring...nothing to tell at the spring..."

Pyttel's sinful act hung over us, between us, but he was a man like any other, and I could not condemn him. I leaned close to his ear and whispered, "Hold your tongue before you condemn yourself."

He covered his mouth with his hand and nodded several times. He understood I would keep his secret—as long as he stayed loyal to me.

The King walked around the nithing horse several times, his face blustering. He thrust the Holy Spear into its hide and ripped it and the skull off the pole. They fell in a heap at his feet. "This is how the rebel attempts to defeat me—with heathen magic and intimidation? The trickery of a coward?" He stomped on the skull, crushing and pounding it into the mud. "This is what remains of the old gods in my kingdom." He panted, his anger spent.

*Destroyed...yet alive*
*Watching me*

When the King had caught his breath, he tried to read the runes carved on the pole. "Brother Pyttel, do you have knowledge of runes?"

"They say Wodan, destruction...and dead man," I said.

"And the rebel bastard set the most ancient and powerful hex at me!" The King handed the Holy Spear to Pyttel then grasped the hefty curse pole. He heaved and groaned, trying to pull out the heavy timber until his entire neck and face were red. Finally, it loosened. One more tug freed it, and he hurled it into the woods. It crashed into a tree. "He will live to regret this and will beg for God's mercy before this is over, I swear by all that is holy!"

"I know where he hides and I have discovered some of those who support and protect him," I said. "He travels across the wilds from farmstead to village, spreading the word of your new laws and the tithe. He is using them to stir up anger and rebellion amongst the peasant freemen and the half-free. The peasants also speak of nobles who have made oaths to you but secretly support rebellion."

"Which Saxon nobles?"

"They avoid mentioning names."

The King scowled and grunted. "Clever heathen swine."

"I have also found the way to the Externsteine. It is less than a day's march from here."

The King's face flushed again. "I knew Sidag was lying to me. But no one else can hear of his treachery. I must catch him in more lies, and others must witness it too. Am I understood, Brother Pyttel?"

He nodded hastily. "Of course, My King."

"What defenses does this place have?" the King asked.

"Pagan ones," I said. "The forest is bewitched to confuse and snare intruders, and the stones are hidden by a heavy mist. There is also a treacherous bog that pulled me into its depths, and thickets of thorny hawthorn that rip apart flesh."

"The witch's bloom," the King mused, tilting his head, searching me for deception. "They say no Christian man can breach the defenses of the Externsteine, but you appear whole enough. I see no torn flesh."

"Gerwulf is only half Christian," said Pyttel.

"Yes, he is." The King nodded with a slight curl to his

lips. "Was Widukind there?"

"The surrounding woodland is heavily patrolled by Wulf-hednar, and his scent was strong there."

The King rubbed his chin, deliberating, then said, "You are the only one who knows the location of the Externsteine and the secrets of the Teutoburg Forest. You will serve as a guide for a raiding party to bring the rebel in—alive."

I disliked the idea. "Dead is quicker—and easier," I said. "I could do that by myself and no one need know of your dealings with me."

"I deal with whomever I will."

"No one will follow me into the Teutoburg Forest," I said. "They would as likely try to kill me…and they would fail."

"No one will know who you are. You are not to use your name or refer to your past," he said.

"That should be simple," Pyttel said. "He says few words."

"But *your* mouth never stops, monk," said the King. "You *will* keep this confidence. Gerwulf will be known as an expert tracker, from the mountains…the Alps far to the south. That is all anyone will be told."

"Yes, My King. So what are we to call him?"

"He will need a name…a Christian name would be best."

"Tracker will suit," I said.

He thought a moment. "So be it," he said.

"What about the wolf skin?" asked Pyttel. "He should leave it behind."

I lifted my lip in a snarl. "No."

The King eyed me for a moment. "Keep it," he said. "But do not invoke the Wulfhedinn in front of the others unless absolutely necessary, and in that case, you had better return with Widukind in irons."

I nodded.

He continued. "My top general, Theoderic, will lead the party. It will include the Saxon nobles Hessi and Sidag. Bringing in Widukind will test their loyalty to me and show Sidag's true nature. You will report how well they aided in this mission. Prince Pepin and Brother Pyttel will also go."

The monk's face fell. "But, Sire. I am a man of God."

"You were also a soldier, and you know these heathens better than anyone else," he said. "Widukind must be made to submit to me and to God, and the entire Frankish Kingdom must know of it. You leave tomorrow."

It was of no use to argue further with him. The King determined that the raiding party would gather a short distance outside the camp palisade at nightfall. He and Pyttel returned to camp, and I found a quiet spot away from Wodan's Spring to rest. As I drifted to sleep, I realized that I had forgotten to mention the woman who rode with Widukind.

# Tracker

⁓

I dozed lightly, warming my bones in the sun until a shadow crossed my face. I smelled rain, and dark heavy clouds moved over the forest. It started to sprinkle, and I took shelter under an oak tree. Soon it poured—a hard shower that would wash away any trace of Widukind.

Waiting for the rain to pass, I focused on the practical matter at hand. Picking up Widukind's trail would have been difficult enough without a storm and the burden of the King's raiding party. I was no nursemaid for a young prince—a cripple—and the King would certainly hold me responsible if Pepin was killed or seriously injured.

What bothered me the most were the Saxon nobles, Hessi and Sidag. I did not trust them—and neither did the King. He was only sending them on this mission to prove their shaky loyalty to him. Worst of all, everyone except Pyttel would likely despise me. The King was wise in sending him with us, but I would have preferred doing this by myself.

The shower lightened to a drizzle, leaving a mist that obscured everything within a few paces. The soaking I got was worth it; I could easily lose my unwanted party in the heavy fog if I chose.

I went early to the meeting place, a clearing outside the palisade, beyond the sight of the guards. Pyttel arrived soon afterward.

"Gerwulf—I mean Tracker!" He was almost unrecognizable. A cap covered his tonsured head, and he wore breeches, a tunic, and a mantle instead of the monk's habit. His seax was sheathed at his side, and he carried a spear and a round shield. Was he the same man? I wondered if the madness would show itself more or less in this attire.

The King soon rode up with his hunchbacked son. "This is my eldest, Pepin," he said without mentioning the boy's title as prince. "He is sturdier than he appears. His mind is brilliant, and his deformity has toughened his character."

"I need no special treatment," he said, his voice stronger than I expected.

"Good. I do not coddle," I said.

"My father says you are the best tracker in the kingdom."

"You will keep up, or I will leave you in the forest," I said.

Pepin's stunned expression told me that no one ever talked to him in this way. Karl's face remained flat while he waited for his son's response.

"I will," Pepin said, trying to square his crooked shoulders. "I am a warrior."

His father broke into a grin. "You see? I do not breed weaklings, and my firstborn is tougher than all the rest."

Pepin beamed.

The Saxon Counts arrived on horseback with General Theoderic leading the way. His expression was hard, like ice; he was too busy calculating his next move to be disturbed by emotion.

Count Hessi rode behind, accompanied by a dozen foot soldiers. He wore a silk mantle dyed saffron yellow—the color of cowards. He was the only one to wear such impractical garments. The General, second in power only to the King, had outfitted himself in a simple leather coat, practical for stealing through thick brush.

Hessi's eyes narrowed and lingered with distaste on my wolf skin, bare chest, and feet. "This barbarian is our guide?" he sneered.

*A low growl*
*Deep in my chest*
*I would leap at him*
*…his fleshy throat, an apple ripe for my jaws*

The King glared at Hessi. "This is Tracker," he said. "He is a highly skilled scout and woodsman. I summoned him from the south mountains to do what none of *you* have accomplished yet. In one night, he has tracked Widukind and found the Externsteine."

"Impossible," said Count Sidag. "It does not exist."

Count Hessi narrowed his eyes. "I told you all that it does exist, but I refuse to take orders from the likes of him."

General Theoderic had remained quiet, listening and watching then took a commanding breath. "No, you will all take your orders from me," he said. "It will be as your King commands, and he decrees that Tracker is guiding this mission."

Hessi's cheeks burned red with humiliation. He sneered. "So be it."

I despised how they spoke of me, as if I was invisible.

*The hackles rise*
*I am here*
*Calling the wolf*
*I live and breathe*
*And I will rip out your throat to prove it…*

Pyttel was observing me. He winked and began to mumble. Through his madness, I understood his words well enough. "We must submit to God…fight for our souls…I tell you. God has said this is our trial…fight for your soul…"

*The beast fades*
*…and all is quiet in my heart*

He knew me well enough now to sense when the wolf was close, and he knew how to deter it. He was as crafty as he was mad.

Hessi rolled his eyes. "Must we tolerate this lunatic as well?"

"Brother Pyttel is touched by God and is an accomplished soldier," said the King. "You will likely be glad of his company before this is over."

Hessi scowled, reining his horse around. "Then let us ride and be done with this."

"There will be no horses," I said, "and no entourage."

Hessi was incensed. "I am a *Count*. I do not trudge about like a common foot soldier."

"We must travel lightly on foot, cutting straight through

the thickest parts of the forest," I said.

Pepin leered at Hessi and slid off his mount. He moved more nimbly with his crooked back and gangly limbs than I expected. "*I* can travel on foot," he said. "You can stay behind Hessi—if you are too old to get your fat arse off your fat horse."

The King smiled under his moustache.

General Theoderic dismounted. "Our Prince has spoken. We go on foot."

Sidag followed suit, but Hessi scowled and made a show of his great displeasure before dismounting.

As the attendants took their mounts, the King leaned toward me and spoke softly. "My son has much to learn, but he will be of use to you, far more use than Hessi and Sidag."

The King returned to camp with Hessi's attendants and the horses. As we prepared to leave, General Theoderic pulled me aside.

"The King and Brother Pyttel have confidence in your skills," he said. "That is *not* enough for me."

I met his sharp gaze. "I would rather hunt down Widukind alone and cut his throat myself."

"As would I," he said, "but this is far more complicated than that. The King wants him captured alive, and we are burdened with the Saxon Counts, who I do not trust. Fortunately, Brother Pyttel has skill with a seax, and his loyalty is solid."

*The man of God who eats the goat's heart at the pagan spring*
*My little secret…*

The general crossed his arms. "You claim you have tracked Widukind to the Externsteine?"

"Yes."

"The King tells me you encountered Wulfhednar there."

"At least a dozen patrols the woods around the stones."

He weighed my words, scratching his chin before speaking again. "What is your plan?"

"We would leave at dusk, staying off the paths that are used by bandits. If I do not pick up Widukind's trail quickly, we will travel straight through the forest to a nearby village east of here. I have tracked him there before, and the villagers support him. By day, they claim faith in God and loyalty to the King; by night they worship the old gods. They have harbored Widukind in the past and rally for an uprising.

"Their village is unprotected, and I can slip through under cover of darkness to learn more. They may be harboring Widukind now, or they might discuss his location or his plans. Our next step will depend on what I learn there."

General Theoderic blinked. It seemed the first time he had done so.

"We go at dusk," he said.

# Nothing Left to Lose

After sunset I led the small contingent into the Teutoburg Forest. The fog lifted slowly, and by nightfall the rising half-moon provided some light. I failed to pick up a fresh scent of Widukind, so I cut through the brush toward the Saxon village.

I kept a fast pace. Behind me, the awkward footsteps of my troop kicked and crushed every branch and tree root. After several miles, I heard one of them stumble, and then Hessi swore.

I worried that their clumsiness had announced our presence. I was sorely tempted to run as the wolf until I lost them all, but after another mile, I stopped and waited for them. I was surprised to see that Pepin had followed me most closely.

"I can keep going," said Pepin. "I am twice as tough as those old men."

Pyttel and General Theoderic soon came along, but the Saxon Counts had lagged so far behind that we had to backtrack to find them.

"They are trying to slow us down," I grumbled under my breath.

"Yes, they are," the General said.

When we reached them, Hessi was making a grand show of getting to his feet after having fallen again. He took time to examine his torn tunic sleeve before getting up.

"If we continue in this manner, we will not get within five miles of Widukind without being heard," I whispered to the General.

"I agree," said Pyttel. "We must go on without them."

The General scrutinized the Saxons. "We will make camp for the night," he said.

Hessi groaned. "But who will build the fire now that you have sent my attendants home?"

"There will be no fire to mark us," said the General. "Tracker, find a suitable place."

They began to grumble about the dampness of the night. I was glad to get away from all of them. I followed the scent of game to a small clearing sheltered partially by a thicket. The spring grasses were trampled flat by deer that had used it to spend the night.

I brushed past the branches a few times. They grazed me without sinking into my flesh or strangling my limbs like the branches and vines near the Raven's Stones had done.

We settled in, and everyone pulled out wineskins. No one was interested in eating the cheese and bread that I smelled in their packs. Hessi kept his salted pork hidden—I was sure he would not share that with anyone. They wanted wine more than food, and the young Pepin was happy to join in.

Everyone drank rapidly, except the General who took small,

calculated sips. The slurping was deafening. The tension slowly eased, but they did not talk, joke, or laugh like I had seen other soldiers do.

Pyttel offered me his wineskin. "Some wine, Tracker?" he asked.

I shook my head, refusing to drink with these men. Instead, I kept up my guard, ears perked. Filling their empty bellies so quickly with wine, no one else except perhaps the General would be alert enough to keep watch.

I pulled out a whetstone and began to sharpen my axes. With each stroke, I glared at the others one by one, letting the blade ring before taking the next stroke. They glanced up from their wine nervously, and Pyttel laughed softly to himself.

The General broke the silence first. "Count Hessi," he said. "I understand that you are the one who handed over Widukind's cloak to the King."

"What of it?" he asked shaking his empty wineskin.

"You betrayed your own brother-in-law," he said.

"I am no traitor—if that is what you are implying." He shifted nervously. "I did it to prove my loyalty to the King!"

General Theoderic remained quiet. Hessi searched the General's face, and when he found no reassurance, he jumped up, swaying to keep his balance.

"*Sidag* is the traitor," he snapped. "He keeps ties and communicates with the rebel leader!"

"I only do what I must to negotiate peace," said Sidag, rising clumsily.

Hessi's words began to slur. "Su…su…supporting rebellion is not making peace!"

Pyttel stepped between them, as if he thought to stop their foolishness, but it was too late. Both men were seething.

Sidag puffed up his chest. "What do you know of loyalty, Hessi? You traded the freedom and souls of all Saxons for Frankish wealth and titles. That is not loyalty—and it certainly is not honorable. How can a man without honor be true to anyone?"

Hessi pointed to the sky. "I have proven myself to God, the One True God!"

"Fidelity is easy for you," said Sidag. "You live far away. My lands lie closest to the Franks. *My* clans are those that have suffered the most from the unending border wars, not you and yours, Hessi."

"You…you!" Hessi thrust his finger at Sidag. "Fool…you and your tribe will suffer more by rebelling."

"What more can I suffer?" ask Sidag. "I lost my wife and two sons in the wars, and my last son is now a hostage of the King."

"The King has given you a new wife," said Hessi, "a younger wife who will bear you many more sons. You can only hope they are yours—I hear her legs are quite open, and that's why he gave her to you."

Sidag lunged at him and punched him in the face. Hessi fell to the ground and moaned, holding a bloody nose.

"She will never replace my wife." His voice trembled with bitterness. "And new sons will never replace those I have lost. But what does it all matter now? They are gone, and I have made promises to My King, *God's* king. I will build a church on my lands, on the place where we once worshipped Wodan…but it will never replace the sacred sites we have lost."

His words hung in the air, and the color drained from his face. He had revealed too much.

I thought of the Saxon bandits—the starving peasants I

had killed. For a moment, I pitied Sidag and his clans, hating Hessi all the more.

Hessi tried to shake the blood from his hand. "Such talk is heresy—punishable by death under the King's new Saxon laws."

"Do you think I fear death now?" Sidag dropped his shoulders and sat down hard on the ground. "I have the promise of paradise from the new God, the Almighty."

General Theoderic crossed his arms with satisfaction. He had cleverly baited them and had heard all he needed from Sidag.

"Forgive me, General Theoderic," Sidag said hurriedly. "My grief for my family is so great...I say things I do not mean. I would like to seek Penance and Reconciliation with Brother Pyttel."

"No, not here," said the General. "You will wait until we return to a proper church. Now we will rest and continue this mission at dawn."

Sidag's face clouded as he wrapped himself in his mantle and lay down. The rest followed, except me, remaining awake, sharpening my axes. Hessi and Sidag shifted restlessly to the sound of the whetstone against the axe blades, but I continued until the edges were keen. Finally, I dragged them against a leather belt until they gleamed.

When I was finished, the night fell quiet. I stayed on guard. After several hours, General Theoderic rose.

"Sleep now," he whispered. "I will take over."

I thought to argue with him, but he was determined. I lay awake, listening to the camp. Hessi and the monk snored loudly, but Sidag and the General breathed lightly—awake. After another hour, Sidag stirred. I peeked through half-closed lids and saw that the General had nodded off. Sidag rose and slipped into the forest.

I jumped up to follow, but the General sat up and shook his head. Then I understood—he had feigned sleep to tempt Sidag to run off.

"Give him a short lead then follow," he said. "See if he runs to Widukind."

# Death was Calling

Count Sidag headed northwest, directly toward the Raven's Stones. I pulled up the wolf hood, unconcerned with the enchanted bog, vines, and thickets that surrounded the stones. I was prepared this time.

*The wolf rises*
*I peer through the beast's eyes*
*Its beating heart, a hammer against my ribs*
*Pounding harder and harder*
*Muscles surge*
*Strength rules*
*Nose up*
*Ears cocked*
*Alert, vigilant*

Sidag's trail was easy to follow. I pursued, closing the gap between us. He was no Wulfhedinn warrior, but his loyalty to Widukind was now certain.

I slowed my pace and crouched low, padding softly. As we came closer to the stones and entered the thickest part of the forest, I stayed alert to vines and thorny thickets. I tested every step for boggy ground before treading. They would not catch me again in their traps.

A chill crept down the back of my neck. I glanced over my shoulder then tried to pick up Sidag's trail, but it had gone cold. The path of crushed grass was gone, and no trace of his scent lingered. He had been only a couple dozen paces ahead of me. How could I have lost him, as slow and clumsy as he was?

*A shriek echoes through the forest*
*Like ice on my neck*
*Like death on my shoulder*

*The wind rises*
*…carrying the scent of sweet musk and hawthorn…*

*The shield maiden appears, tall atop her mount*
*Raven's head and woman's breasts*
*Black banner waving behind*
*Extending wider*
*Stretching into wings*
*Poised to take flight*

*Her beak drips blood onto my tongue*
*I hunger for it…*
*Bring it to me*

*Her great horse paws the grounds and throws its head*
*My long axe swings wide*
*…around and around…*
*She aims her spear and spurs*
*Eyes burning red as fire*
*She charges*
*Hooves shaking the ground*

*You will not take me*

*Hooves pounding*
*Axe swinging wide*
*Around and around*
*End this…end it now…*

*Her wings flap…once, twice, three times*
*Climbing into the sky*
*…and the Raven soars above…*

Footsteps approached. Pyttel burst from the brush, seax drawn. "What was that?"

"What are you doing here, monk?" I demanded.

"God sent me to you."

"You tracked *me?*"

"…that scream. I have never heard anything like it."

I scoured the night sky, but it was empty. A single black feather floated down to the ground. I stepped on it, burying it in the mud. "Just a rabbit caught by a fox."

He shivered. "That was no dying rabbit! It sounded like… death was calling my name."

"I warned you not to listen to her…"

"*Her?* Is it the spirit of a woman? Did you see her?"

"Ask me no more!" I said. "Return to your church. Do your penance and pray to God for forgiveness of your sins. Stay away from Wodan's Spring and these woods."

"I must confront the Saxon spirits and their gods if I am to save them."

"They have already beaten you," I said. "They have stolen your mind."

"Yes, I am mad—mad enough to have confronted *you*."

I faltered, turned away, and started walking. "Go home, monk."

"If I leave now, you may never return."

I moved on, and he tagged along.

Something felt different. I kept going, trying to understand what had changed. Was it the forest? Was it merely the monk's presence?

I tried to pick up Sidag's scent and failed. I cut northeast, in the general direction of the Raven's Stones, but the terrain was unfamiliar. After another hour, I realized that I had forgotten to pull up the wolf's hood. I reached for it, finding it already on my head, pulled low over my face, but it lay on my head like an ordinary hood, and the wolf had stayed away. I began to think the monk's holy presence was working against me.

"Is she nearby—the spirit?" Pyttel asked.

"Go home, monk."

Birds were beginning to sing. By the time dawn broke, I had not found a trace of Sidag or Widukind and was completely unsure in which direction the stones lay. Daylight did not help, and I was frustrated and exhausted.

Pyttel yawned. "We are walking in circles. Admit it, you have lost him."

I growled low and glared. Instead of recoiling, he yawned again, and soon I yawned too. I found a dry place, drew my skin around me, and bedded down.

Pyttel glanced around. "What does she look like, the spirit?" he asked.

"A raven."

He fell to his knees, holding his cross aloft. "The Eater of Souls! My Lord God! No, no! I tell you it is over...no more... my killing time is over, but she comes for me...to gorge on my blood and carry my soul to Hell. Help me to stay strong in faith lest the Death Angel takes me now, before my penance is done!"

Why had I told him about the Raven? Maybe I thought the answer would silence him.

"Shut up monk. She has not come for you. She feasts on me."

"Pray with me, Wulfhedinn! Plead for God to watch over us," he said. "I beseech the Lord! Protect us from the Eater of Souls until all our sins have been forgiven...I beseech the Lord..."

He repeated it over and over until I kicked him. He rolled onto his side and was quiet. As I drifted to sleep, I heard him again. He started slowly, breathing heavily, steadily in rhythm— with his hand on his cock. I wished he would start babbling again, and then he did.

"...is over...is over...is over...," he panted.

I threw a stick at him, turned over, and let him finish.

# Thy Will Be Done

We rose at midday.

Pyttel got up stiffly, rubbed his back, and moaned. "I have become an old man," he said, "but I am still here." He cackled, content and pleased with himself then raised his wineskin in toast and drained the last few drops.

We ate the bread and cheese he carried.

"Will you try to pick up Sidag's trail again?" he asked, licking his fingers.

"Yes."

"After we find him, I want you to take me to the Raven's Stones."

"I plan on losing you today."

He grinned, making it clear that he was determined to stay.

We set out. The wolf did not rise, and Pyttel kept up with me all day. By dusk, I still had found no trace of Sidag, Widukind, or the stones. The Raven had vanished as well, yet I felt as if they were all nearby.

We stopped to rest. Pyttel's lips parted, on the verge of talking about the Raven, but he wisely remained quiet. It made me suspicious, but I was too hungry to think about it. I caught two rabbits, and we skinned and roasted the little carcasses.

"Ah, meat!" He smacked his lips and wiped his mouth with his hand as he ate. "Monastery food is vile—too many boiled beans and vegetables. Fortunately, the King favors roasted meat at court." He sat back, belched, and picked his teeth. "We have walked in circles long enough. You have obviously lost Sidag, and it is time to report back to the King."

"I have nothing to bring him yet," I said.

"Maybe you are losing your touch, Wulfhedinn."

I jumped up and threw my francisca as hard as I could at a tree. My aim was poor, and it fell to the ground with an unsatisfying thud.

He laughed. "This may be a good sign for you. Either way, it is time to return to court. General Theoderic and Count Hessi will have returned by now. Hessi hates you and will likely tell the King that you have deserted, and it is impossible to tell how the General feels about anyone. He is cunning, and he probably suspects who you really are. What if he blames you for Sidag's escape to cover his own failure as leader of the mission?"

"You fool, the General let Sidag go, hoping he would lead me to Widukind."

"Oh," he said, clearing his throat. "Regardless, your loyalty will be in question unless we return soon."

"None of it matters if I return without Sidag and Widukind—or at least some news of their whereabouts."

"Now is not the right time to continue," he said.

"Is God telling you this again?" I asked. "God does not talk to monks who kill better than they pray."

His face fell, and he knotted his brow. "This I do know, Wulfhedinn..." His voice had an edge I had not heard before. "I am your *only* connection to God now—and he favors me, as does the King. If you truly seek to vanquish the Eater of Souls and return to the world of men, you must keep faith with me. If you do this, I swear to you...thy will be done."

He was right. I had nowhere else to go—except back to the domain of the Raven.

*Every night unchanged*
*Alone with her when darkness falls*
*The morning sun blinding me*
*Chasing me into the shadows*
*Another night, another day*
*Lost to the Raven*

*I could bear her no longer*
*Submit to God*

The next morning, I returned with Pyttel to the King's garrison at Lippespringe. It was a distance I could have covered in an hour running as the wolf, but I took my time, dragging my feet. I detoured several times, hoping to pick up a trace of Sidag or Widukind.

Pyttel was patient until I heard his stomach growl.

"Let us return to the King's camp before dinner and get some real food," he said.

Getting hungry myself, I relented, but every step back to camp was heavy with frustration. The air near the camp remained clear of ashy smoke, and it was quiet—too quiet. Nobody travelled the road, and no guards patrolled the walls. The camp appeared deserted.

Pyttel and I glanced at each other. He lent me his mantle to cover my skin, and we walked straight through the unbarred gate. Little remained of the garrison but trampled mud, midden piles, and horse shit. A single crushed ox cart missing a wheel lay on its side in the middle of it all.

"The King has retreated," I said.

It began to rain, and Pyttel pulled his cap back on and pulled it low over his face. "King Karl does not retreat," he said. "He pulls back to plan and muster more forces."

A few people scavenged through the kitchen middens, and a dozen others spread across the field where the soldier's tents had been staked. They picked through the mud, oblivious to the rain. A man near us found a small knife and wiped it on his filthy tunic.

"What has happened here?" Pyttel asked him.

The man eyed us suspiciously. "Who are you?" His voice was raspy, and he was missing most of his teeth.

"I am Brother Pyttel, scholar and assistant to Alcuin, the King's advisor and teacher of his court. This is my…assistant." He nodded toward me.

"More dirty foragers." He pointed a stump of a finger that had been cut off at the middle knuckle. "This is *my* area. Find somewhere else."

Pyttel raised his voice. "Where did the army go?"

"Away."

Pyttel pulled a silver half-denier out of the pouch at his waist.

The forager's face lit up. "The great and mighty King has moved to that fine palace of his at Paderborn," he said and spat.

"With the entire army?"

He spread his arms. "Do you see them here?"

"What else have you heard?"

He gawked at the coin, scratching his crotch absentmindedly. "The King's Holy Spear was stolen," he said.

Pyttel's face darkened. "*Stolen?*"

"Some say it was those pig-shit Saxons, the ones the King has made noble—greedy, lying thieves, the lot of 'em."

Pyttel tossed the silver to the ground.

He snatched it up, unheeded by his missing finger. "I *could* tell you much more—things that are dangerous to repeat," he said, his sight fixed on Pyttel's coin pouch.

Pyttel pulled out another coin. The forager tried to grab the coin, but Pyttel gave it to me, and he backed down.

"Some say it was stolen by a wolf demon that roams the Teutoburg Forest—a Wulfhedinn."

Pyttel and I exchanged looks.

"A Wulfhedinn?" asked Pyttel. "Who says such things?"

"Many do, but if you ask me, our holy King got what he deserved...making pacts with those dirty Godless heathens. He is dealing with the Devil when he should slaughter the lot of 'em."

We left him to rummage through the remains of the camp. I thought of the King with his thick muscles, his temper enraged like a lion.

*The Raven perches on the broken ox cart*
*Rain dripping off her sleek black wing*
*She shakes out her feathers*
*Tilts her head at me*

*Return to the wilds*
*I hunger*

"I would be a fool to go within ten miles of the King now," I said.

"But you *must* return to clear your name," Pyttel said. "I will bear witness that you have been with me and could not possibly be the thief."

"The King will spike my head before you can open your mouth."

"No. He will listen to me. I am his confessor and have interceded with God to pardon all of his wicked secrets—and he has more than most."

"Why is it so easy for a King to find redemption?" I asked.

"Because he is arrogant, and remorse weighs lightly on him." His gaze followed mine to the ox cart. "You see her again, the Eater of Souls?"

"No," I lied. "It is only a raven."

# Grace Dwells
in the Deed

⌇⌇⌇

J did not know why I followed Pyttel, but I did. Maybe if I
stayed with him long enough, the Raven would leave me.

We took the Hellweg to Karlsburg Palace at Paderborn. It
ran southwest along the Lippe River and bore evidence of the
hasty retreat of a large army. Horses, wagons, and people had
trampled the rain-soaked ground into an impassible mire. We
were forced to skirt through the forest to cover the six miles to
the palace.

Pyttel was quiet. It made me edgier than when he babbled.

"I tell you this…" he said suddenly. "Whoever returns the
Holy Spear to the King will be able to name their reward, in
this life and the next."

We found high ground where we could see over the timber wall surrounding Paderborn. Every bit of space inside was
jammed with wattle buildings, lean-to huts, and army tents.
The rain had chased most people inside, except the soldiers

patrolling the walls, pulling their mantles close about them.

The King's stone palace rose above it all at the far end of town. The palace included a great hall that stood ten times the height of a man. It was partially enclosed by a tall whitewashed wall that glistened in the rain.

"It is no wonder the King retreated here," I said.

"He is bringing civilization to the pagan wilds." Pyttel's voice was crisp, cynical. "This might be his largest palace yet when it is done, certainly the most fortified. In any case, I must report to him alone. With the spear stolen, he will be in a foul temper—probably the worst I have ever seen—and we are not bringing him good news." He shuddered. "I will try to convince him of your innocence. Wait for me here."

I was glad to stay outside town by myself for a while. I needed time to breath without hearing anyone's chattering.

The rain stopped, and the townspeople emerged from indoors. Carpenters returned to sawing and hammering, and masons cut stone to complete the wall around the palace. Their voices and laughter floated over the walls to me. I wondered what they said to make each other laugh. I kicked a rock and wandered a short distance into the woods where the air was fresher.

> *The light blinds, chasing me into the shadows*
> *And the Raven floats on warm currents*
> *Wandering farther*
> *I lead, and she follows*
> *Drawn deeper…farther*
> *She leads, and I follow*
> *Darkness falling*

*Come, Wulfhedinn*
*Stay with me*
*I hunger*


I stopped to relieve myself, tempted to linger. It was a luxury—too easy to be caught off guard while pissing. I pulled up my breeches and heard something so subtle that I had to cock my head to the side to be sure of it.

It grew louder and more distinct...the clomping of hooves and three voices. They drew nearer. I ducked behind the brush, glimpsing them through the branches as they approached—three Scola riders, well-equipped with swords, shields, and armor. Their horses moved slowly, picking their way through the untracked woodland. They did not appear to be patrolling so far off the road, and they lacked dogs for hunting.

"I tell you this," said one of the soldiers. He was a giant of a man that dwarfed his mount, its back sagging under the strain. "He is possessed with hellfire. You should have seen his face, red and twisted. I thought his eyes would burst from his head! He destroyed his entire tent and threw axes at his personal guards."

They all laughed.

"...as if the Holy Spear would reappear simply by his command!" said another soldier. He wore burly scale armor and had a whey-face under his iron helmet. "He does not suspect us... does he?"

"You are a gutless weasel," said the giant. "He suspects *everyone*. Stiffen your spine. It cannot be undone now."

The weasel lowered his shoulders and was silenced—not all Scolas were as threatening as they appeared to be.

"*I* would do it again," said the third soldier, a gangly man. "I am sick of risking my life in the heathen wilds for the pride of a self-rutting maniac. The booty for us ran dry long ago in Saxony..."

"So today we reap our well-deserved reward," said the giant.

So some of the Scolas had stolen the Holy Spear; I was not surprised; they were nobles with access to the King and the spear—and they were arrogant enough to do it. They were likely in league with Sidag or other nobles, either Frank or Saxon or both. There were many who resented the King and coveted the relic.

...and now, it had fallen into my path.

I trailed them through the forest toward the King's abandoned camp on the Lippe River. By sunset, they had skirted the walls and continued beyond, deep into the woods. It was dark when they dismounted at a large fallen tree, partly covered by brush. I grabbed the snout of my hood and pulled it low.

*Crouched, motionless*
*The wolf returns!*
*Its beating heart steals inside, pounding harder and harder*
*Muscles surge*
*Strength rules*
*Watching and waiting...*

The weasel pulled away fallen branches, revealing a hollow trunk. He knelt and pulled out a hide—a wolf hide. He threw it over his head, growled weakly, and jumped around.

"That thing stinks!" The gangly soldier laughed and held his nose. "Get rid of it."

"It has done its job well," the giant said. "The gossips spread the word of a Wulfhedinn thief quicker than I expected."

The weasel dropped the hide and reached into the hollow

again. The giant shoved him aside and pulled out a spear—the Holy Spear.

"We should keep it for ourselves," said the weasel.

"No, Widukind is paying us well enough for it," said the giant.

I had heard enough.

*The wolf howls*
*A long snapping, snarling shriek...*

The soldiers glanced around and drew their swords. They were ripe for ambush. No armor, no weapon would shield them now.

"What was that?"

"A wolf," said the giant. "Get back on your horses."

"I have never heard a wolf like that," said the weasel.

*Trotting though the trees*
*Rustling underbrush*
*Cracking twigs*
*Growling and yelping*

They started, twisting in their saddles, squinting to try to see through the thick cover.

The gangly soldier pointed. "It is over there now!"

The weasel pointed in the other direction. "I heard it from over there...there is more than one!"

"Stay together and move forward," the giant said.

I circled around them.

*A long snapping, snarling shriek*
*Then another…and another*
*Ring of fear*
*Squall of death*

"Those are no wolves," said the gangly soldier.

The weasel reined his horse between the other two. "They are all around us—demons!" he squealed. "They are hunting us…for stealing the Holy Spear!"

"There is nothing to fear." The giant held the Holy Spear aloft. "We have the weapon of God."

Of the three, the giant was the biggest threat. I moved to a spot with a clear view of him and hefted my francisca. Holding my breath, I threw. It spun through the air and ripped through his throat. He fell, the Holy Spear landing next to his body.

*A long snapping, snarling shriek*
*Then another…and another*
*Ring of fear*
*Squall of death*

The horses reared and whinnied. The weasel tried to hang on but was thrown, landing with a hard thud. I leapt at him from the brush, long axe swinging…around and around. One chop through the neck—a quick death.

The gangly soldier regained control of his mount and raised his sword. His long jaw trembled at the sight of his fallen comrades, blood pumping from their necks. He froze. I charged, swinging…around and around, but he did not move.

"God save me from the demon…"

I swung at his leg and it fell, his body tumbling with it. One swing at his neck, and his head rolled.

*The wolf growls*
*Rising from deep within the chest*
*From the heart*
*Fury born of pain*

Their skulls splintered under my blade.

*And the Raven comes to feast*

I snatched up the Holy Spear and escaped deeper into the forest. My heart pounding, I clenched it tightly and ran madly without direction until exhaustion overtook me.

Panting…gasping for air, I steadied my trembling fingers on the rough shaft. They reached to touch the blade that pierced the Lord's ribs, His spilt blood almost alive on the tip.

I dropped to my knees and folded my hands around it in prayer—the first prayer to God in many years. Would he hear me now? My mouth moved, but blessed words failed…

The wolf skin—it clung to me, foul and stinking of my sins. I jumped up, tore it off, and tried to pray again.

*He calls*
*In a soft voice that flows like water over rocks*
*God is calling me…*
*From a stream at the edge of the clearing*

I rose and stumbled across the field to the bank of the stream and fell again to my knees.

*God's voice fades*
*…and the wolf wails*

*Peering at me from the water*
*Panting, tongue hangs over bloody fangs*
*Masking my face*

*The Raven looms over my shoulder*
*She cackles*
*I hunger*

*Feed the wolf*
*Feed the Raven*

I slapped at the water to destroy the image. The relic slipped from my hand, and I collapsed. I lay there, my face buried in my hands. I did not know how much time passed, but I awoke to darkness, curled up with the wolf skin.

*The stream speaks*
*Words flowing like water over rocks*
*Words I have heard before*

*You cannot invoke God with magic…*
*Grace dwells not in the spear, but in the deed*
*Fight for your soul*

I stood. The dried blood was so thick on my skin that it cracked. I took a step into the icy stream. My heart leaped into my throat. I dove in, layers of filth washing off, streaming around me. I emerged from the water and grabbed the spear with cold, numb fingers. I hesitated then threw the skin over my back and ran to the palace.

# Speak Only of God

I sprinted to Paderborn, my wet body drying quickly. A clear route unfolded ahead of me through the thick forest. The air was fresh, the earth soft under my feet as I leapt over logs and dodged under branches. I was bringing the King his precious spear.

The deed—it was all that mattered now.

I scanned overhead and behind, listening, smelling. Widukind and his Wulfhednar were likely close, waiting for the Frankish traitors to bring them the spear, but I did not smell them. The Raven had also vanished. There was no pounding of hooves behind me—no scent of sweet musk and hawthorn. God was smiling on me.

I stopped and dropped to my knees, making the sign of the cross. I raised the spear aloft, arms stretching wide, and found the words to pray, "Holy Father in heaven, thank you for providing me with the opportunity to prove myself worthy of your grace."

The words sounded so strange, but I did not dwell on it and looked forward to presenting the Holy Spear to the King. I pictured how Pyttel's mangled forehead and crushed nose would twist in surprise when I appeared with the Holy Spear.

I returned to the hill near Paderborn where Pyttel had left me.

He was there, dressed as a monk again, pacing frantically. "Where have you been?" His jaw dropped, and his voice rose with excitement. "The spear...could it be....?" He reached for it. "Where...how...?"

"The King must be the first to know," I said.

"Yes, yes, of course," he agreed. "This is great news! You see? God was with you! This will bring us all great blessings. The King was in such a temper. At first, he refused to see me, and when he finally did, he threw his wine glass at me. He did not want to see you at all, but this changes everything!"

He embraced me tightly. "Were the thieves Saxons?" he asked in my ear. "Frankish traitors? Someone in high ranking at court must have helped them."

I pulled away from him. "Stop asking, lest I ask you about your sacrilege at Wodan's Spring.

He scowled. "Whatever brought you to this miracle," he said suspiciously, "never, *ever* tell the King about Wodan's Spring or the Eater of Souls."

"I will speak only of God."

"Yes, God indeed," he said. "Let us speak only of God."

# To Take a Piss

―――⁓―――

**P**yttel led us to the town's gate. "You look better," he commented. "Did you bathe?"

"I got wet."

"You could have stayed in the water a little longer," he said. "In any case, there is no need to sneak around anymore. With the Holy Spear in hand, you are untouchable—but I will do the talking."

He shouted to the guard, "Open the gate! It is Brother Pyttel. Open the gate for the blessed Holy Spear! It has returned to God's King!"

Several guards peeked over the wall, and the gates opened.

Inside, the Captain of the guard confronted us. He scrutinized me until his eyes fell on the spear. He swallowed deeply and lifted his hand slightly as if to touch it. I tightened my grip, sure he would try to take it.

"How do I know this is the...?"

"I am a man of God and have held the Holy Spear many times," said Pyttel. "I know it when I see it."

"Of course, Brother, but who is this?" He glared at me.

I stepped toward him.

*The wolf calls*
*Aching to jump*

Brother Pyttel put a calming hand on my shoulder. "He is a tracker working for the King. He has retrieved the spear from the thieves."

"I know nothing of a tracker."

"Do you think the King tells *you* everything he does?"

The Captain scoffed then touched the spear's shaft. "Well, this is great news indeed."

By this time many of the guards had gathered around us, gawking at the spear. The Captain led a detachment to accompany us to the palace. We walked through the muddy lanes toward the palace. Everyone, including the blacksmiths, stopped what they were doing and stared. A crowd gathered and word spread through the narrow streets.

"The Holy Spear! The relic has been returned!"

"God be praised!"

People fell to their knees and made the sign of the cross as we passed. Some pushed through the crowd to try to touch it. I glared at them, and they startled and backed away, muttering.

"Who is that with the spear?"

"Filthy!"

"...an animal!"

"Why is *he* holding it?"

*The wolf moans*
*Aching to jump*

Pyttel leaned over, put his arm around my shoulders, and whispered, "Do not listen to them. You have the Holy Spear. Soon, everything will change."

*The wolf retreats*

I was glad when we entered the palace gate and left the town behind. The Captain spoke with the palace guards, and they took us to the King's chamber.

King Karl was pouring over a table of maps with General Theoderic, Chamberlain Adalgis, and Gallo the Horse Master.

"My King." Pyttel bowed deeply. "Forgive me for this interruption…"

The King's eyes flashed then locked onto the spear. He pushed aside Adalgis and grabbed it from me. He examined it carefully and broke into a huge grin.

"Well done!" He slapped me on the back. "Well done. I was right to trust you."

Adalgis' and Gallo's jaws dropped open, but General Theoderic did not appear surprised.

Adalgis collected himself. "Are you sure it is the *real* relic?" He went to the King's side to inspect it. "There are many forgeries."

"Do not question me!" the King boomed. "I know my own relic!"

Adalgis turned up his nose. "And who is this savage that brings it to you?"

"He is a tracker from the Bavarian Alps," the King said.

"I hired him to do what none of you have done. Now get out! Leave me to talk with him."

Pyttel was hiding a grin behind his hand until the King ordered him to leave as well. His face darkened, but he obeyed with the rest.

Once the door closed, the King spoke bluntly. "I am no fool," he said. "I know who stole my spear. Three of my own Scola soldiers had gone missing and were found dead this morning in the forest near the Lippespringe. They were all marked, beheaded cleanly—as if by one swing of an axe. They were mauled nearly beyond recognition—as if attacked by a beast."

He searched my face for a response. I met his gaze with an icy stare.

His upper lip curled into a smirk. "Good. You can hold your tongue, and it is impossible to read your thoughts." He stroked his moustache. "You will need that skill often in my court."

He set the spear against the wall and carefully rolled up his sleeves. He filled his chest with several deep breaths, picked up a bench, and threw it across the room. It hit the stone wall and broke into pieces. "The sow-sucking worms!" Spittle sprayed from his mouth. "This is how I am repaid after the great favor I have shown them!"

He spun around, searching for his next target. He bent and shoved his shoulder under the stone map table.

"Augh!" He grunted, pushing and heaving.

He rocked the table, tipping it up on two legs. It fell back down against his shoulder. He took more deep breaths, the veins in his neck and forehead bulging, and tried again. It tipped farther this time, but not far enough to overturn. Sweat trickled down his cheek, and his face was so red I thought it would burst.

I joined him, pressing my shoulder under the table, and together we tipped it over. It crashed with a boom so loud that it threatened to break through the floor.

"That felt good." He panted, his temper cooling. "Killing them all myself would have felt better. I despise betrayal over all." His voice was now calm and calculated. "I hope you tore them apart slowly." He smirked, rolled down his sleeves, and picked up the spear. "But no matter. They are dead, rotting in Hell. And I have my spear." He ran his hand over the spear tip. "Did you learn anything else from them?"

"They were on their way to sell the spear to the Saxons."

"Widukind?"

"Yes. They talked of a meeting with him."

He frowned. "He still must be close by, but Brother Pyttel told me you were unable to track him—or Sidag."

"I lost them both."

He shrugged. "It is far better that you retrieved my Holy Spear! Yes, yes, far better. I have no doubt that you will find him again after some rest and food—and a bath."

I scowled, but he took no notice.

He continued, "In repayment for this deed, I will see that you receive absolution and are returned to the Church—in secret of course. No one, other than Brother Pyttel and me, is ever to know who—or what—you really are. You will remain a peasant tracker from the south—no one of importance until you brought me my relic."

"Yes," I said, having no desire to tell anyone of my past.

He twisted his magnificent red-gold moustache. "The Externsteine will not stand long now," he said. "I will send you with an entire army to destroy and to drag the coward out of his hole and destroy it…but an army must have a road. Work to extend the Hellweg through the Teutoburg Forest is too slow.

Sidag's peasants have stopped working since he disappeared, and I need my Frankish resources in other places. I will make plans for it soon though, detailed plans, and you will be a critical part of them."

I bowed my head stiffly.

"So, Tracker, how did you come to know of the thieves?"

I looked him in the eye. "I stumbled upon them when I went to take a piss."

He broke into loud, rolling laughter.

# Play His Game

⌒⌒⌒

The King lodged Pyttel and me within his own quarters in the palace and lavished luxury upon us. His servants brought a large helping of roasted meat, bread, and beer and fussed over us as if we were helpless.

One of them wrinkled his nose. "But someone *has* been in the wilds a long time," he said, "and that foul pelt!" He reached to pull it off. "I will get rid of it."

I growled at him. He recoiled and stepped away.

"Not to worry, master groom," said Pyttel. "He will not wear it to court."

The groom took another step back and left with the rest of the servants. The aroma of roasted pork drew me to the table. I sat on a bench and ate. It tasted unlike any other meat; so tender and delicious. I ate until my stomach stretched, and I became sleepy. The only sounds coming from Pyttel's mouth were loud smacking and eating noises.

The servants dragged in a huge wooden tub then filled it with steaming pots of water. When we had finished eating, they tugged at my wolf skin and breeches, trying to undress me for a bath.

I pulled away. "Be gone! I had a bath."

Pyttel rolled his eyes. "The King has sent his personal grooms to attend you," he said. "Let them do their job."

"I can care for myself." I took off the skin, glaring at the grooms then laid it carefully on the table. I felt them staring at my back. I had forgotten. I reached to cover myself with the skin again, but it was too late.

"…your back!" said Pyttel. "What happened…?"

"It is nothing."

I left the skin on the table and dropped my breeches, covering my groin from their prying eyes as I put one foot into the tub. The water was so hot I pulled back immediately. Slowly, I put it back in, then the other leg, and lowered myself, letting the heat soak through my skin into my bones.

Pyttel climbed in, chuckling.

One of the grooms approached me with a scrub brush and ball of herbed soap. I scowled and grunted, startling him. He dropped them in the water and backed away. After I washed myself, he held a large towel, ready to wrap it around me. I grabbed it from him, covering myself as I climbed out of the tub. The grooms surrounded me in a pack with perfumed oil, shears, and a razor.

I veered away. "Enough!" I roared.

Pyttel laughed. "The King is honoring you with this luxury. He is preparing you for a position in his court. He will likely ennoble you."

"Who would want to be a noble?" I recoiled again from one of them.

"To refuse his generosity would be an insult. The good Lord knows you have earned some comforts. Enjoy them. This is all part of His blessing."

I relented and allowed them to shave my beard and cut my hair. When they finished, my face felt naked and my head lighter. One groom pulled a comb through the curly knots and ran his fingers through it, arranging it with great care. Soon, I had had enough. I shook my head, and his work was undone.

Another one attacked my face with tiny pinchers, pulling hair from my brow.

I shoved him away. "Are you trying to blind me?"

"Just taming the fur," he said.

"No more!"

"Very well," he said, holding up a looking glass.

I did not recognize the face staring back at me. The long beard was gone, replaced by a drooping moustache in the style of the Frankish nobles. My hair was neatly clipped to my shoulders.

I was presented with a linen shirt, silk tunic, belt, breeches, and a mantle trimmed in embroidered silk. There were also boots and new linen strips to wrap my feet and lower legs.

They stood up, ready to attend me, but I snatched the clothing and threw on the shirt. It covered my back and was long enough to keep their eyes off my groin. I left the rest.

Pyttel laughed. "All of it," he said.

I put on the breeches.

"The tunic too," he said, "and the boots."

I scowled, and pulled it over my head and buckled the belt. I fumbled to wrap the linen strips around my feet and legs. Pyttel cackled and showed me how to roll them into a neat ball before unwinding them up my leg. The boots came last.

I wanted to tear it all off. The tunic pulled tightly across my chest and shoulders, and the boots squeezed my feet. Sweat beaded on my forehead. I was scrubbed clean but did not feel refreshed, and the tight clothing only magnified the unpleasant feeling.

I gazed again in the looking glass, hoping to catch a glimpse of the wolf. The bare-faced image peered back at me. Who was this man?

The belt began to feel tight, knotting and squeezing…moving up to my chest. I ripped it off.

"What are you doing?" asked Pyttel.

"I cannot wear it."

"That would be ungracious," said Pyttel.

I relented, buckling the King's belt loosely. My face flushed; sweat forming on my upper lip. I wanted to run…had to run.

"Tracker, what is it?" asked Pyttel, standing refreshed in a clean new habit. "You are shaking."

I tugged at the clothing. "I cannot breathe."

"You are breathing," he assured me. "The clothing will take some getting used to, but that will happen. You have confronted the Eater of Souls. Surely, you can manage a silk tunic." He pulled my cross out from under the fabric so it was visible on my chest and patted it. "There. Now you are a noble Christian Frank."

"I must get out of here."

"Come, come to the window and take some fresh air," he said guiding me with a gentle hand.

I went with him and leaned out. We were far above the ground, as though I had climbed a tree. I was tempted to jump out, but Pyttel stood by me, with his hand on my arm until I could breathe again.

I turned from the window, feeling strangely sad.

"You know that running around half naked will no longer

do," said Pyttel. "The King is no fool. He wants to use you to demonstrate his generosity to those who are loyal to him. Yes, he is pleased with you, but he is also making this into an opportunity for himself. You must play his game now."

"Game...?"

"It begins at court this afternoon, then a feast tonight."

"But I just ate enough to last days."

"Nonsense. You are always hungry. Besides, you *must* go. You are the guest of honor—and you have much to learn in little time."

"Learn? What...?"

"Court etiquette—how to eat without looking like an animal."

I scoffed.

"...what to say...what *not* to say." The monk hesitated. "Most importantly, you must also be prepared to give your oath of fealty to the King—in front of the court."

"I swear no oaths."

"Cast those demon eyes away from me!" he said. "You claim that you want God's grace, to return to the Church, and now you must prove it."

"I returned the King's precious holy relic to him! What more must I prove?"

"Your oath to the Christian King is what will make you a man among men, worthy of grace, one of God's flock. Is that not what you want?" he asked.

"Yes," I grumbled. "So teach me the oath."

He nodded. "First, you must learn how to address the King and bow to him at court. You must always address him as My King."

"My...King," I muttered.

"That sounds more like a threat than an acknowledgment

of your King. Lower your head and soften your voice."

I looked at my feet. "My King." The words felt like they were choking me.

"No…no…no. Softer, meekly."

I glared at him, and he stepped back.

"It will get easier," he said. "Submission usually does—usually. Anyway, we will keep practicing."

He taught me the oath of fealty and many other things—how to greet nobles and how to eat with the thumb and middle finger. There were a lot of foolish rules with no purpose, and it was difficult to remember them all.

"At the feast, do not throw bones over your shoulder," said Pyttel. "Do not blow your nose into a neighbor's sleeve or spit in the washing bowl."

The list was endless. "What *can* I do?"

"Be gracious—and for the sake of heaven, stop glaring at people. You have the glower of a madman."

"Who are you to call me a…?"

"And try to smile a bit."

I grinned widely. It made my jaw ache.

"Not so much!" he said. "Do not show so many teeth—it disturbs people."

I dropped the grin and frowned.

"To smile properly, you must imagine something that makes you happy." He closed his eyes, sighed, and the corners of his lips lifted. "Think of a sweet memory."

I did not want to picture what gave him pleasure, but I could think of nothing for myself. Nothing but a scent…

*Sweet musk and hawthorn*

"That is the deepest scowl I have seen yet." Pyttel crossed his arms. "You must have some memory that is pleasant."

"Leave me alone."

"Well, you will not be alone now. All attention will be on you at court and at the feast. The whole palace of Karlsburg and all of Paderborn is talking about you."

I shifted uncomfortably. "Why must they talk about me?"

"Because people need someone and something to talk about." He touched my arm. "Tell me what happened." He licked his lips, anticipating a good story. "The guards are talking about the Scola horsemen who were found dead in the forest. Their heads were chopped cleanly off the bodies and pounded into pulp...the mark of your hand. Were they the thieves? I would have liked to see you do that."

"Shut up, monk!"

Before he could say more, the King burst into the room. He looked past me and paused, blinked, and leaned closer. "Astonishing!" He grinned. "You have been transformed."

Pyttel bowed and nodded his head at me. He wanted me to return the King's smile, but I could not.

The King laughed. "I understand. My groom can be too meticulous—I prefer a simpler style myself—but appearance is crucial for court and tonight's feast. First, you must receive absolution and be reinstated to the Church. Pyttel, take care of it."

Pyttel's jaw dropped. "My King, this would be better done by a bishop."

"You have brought him back to God. You are the best one."

"It should occur on sacred ground, in a church."

"There are too many ears in churches. You will do it now, here. I will serve as witness."

Pyttel took a deep breath. "But, My King..."

"Has he not redeemed himself and shown true repentance

by returning God's Holy Spear to me?"

"He has, Sire."

"Then let this be done."

Pyttel began. "Do you, Tracker, seek reconciliation of your sins in accordance with the rites of God's Holy Church?" he asked.

I knelt and clasped my hands in prayer.

"I do," I said.

"Do you, Tracker, have remorse for all your sinful deeds and the evil you have wrought?"

"I do."

"Do you, Tracker, have the sincere desire to turn from evil and live a virtuous, honorable life and perform good deeds for the glory of God?"

"I do."

"May our Lord Jesus Christ absolve you; and by His authority, I release you from every bond of excommunication and interdict, so far as my power allows and your needs require." He made the sign of the cross. "Thereupon, I absolve you from your sins in the name of the Father, and of the Son, and of the Holy Spirit. Amen."

"Amen," I said. I had not said the affirmation in many years, and it sounded strange—as odd as my new name. "Amen," I repeated, but the word dried up in my mouth.

"It is done," the King said. "Your past no longer exists, and we will not speak of it again." He was staring at my wolf skin on the table.

I reached for it, but Pyttel shook his head.

"Keep it," the King said. "You will need it for what you must do."

# A Man Among Men

I clutched the wolf skin, running my fingers through the fur. My sins were forgiven. I waited for something, a feeling, a sign.

"What does the grace of God feel like?" I asked Pyttel after the King left.

"I cannot tell you that."

"Should I not be feeling something?"

"What did you expect? Choirs of Angels? That God would light the sky with lightning like Donar, the Thunder God?" He pulled the skin out of my hands and set it back down. "You must give it time. Stop brooding. Now is not the time for worry. It is the time to be presented at the court of the King—and drink in celebration!" He winked.

A dozen palace guards escorted us through long passages to the great hall. Their boots padded across the stone floor, changing direction so many times it seemed we were walking in circles. It was no wonder God's grace had lost me in this place.

The doors of the great hall stood three times my height. They opened, creaking under the weight of heavy timber fortified with iron. The grandest hall I had ever seen rose before me. Thick stone walls held the ceiling high in the sky. The King's hall almost touched heaven itself—and I had been invited inside.

Tapestries of red, green and blue decorated brightly painted walls. A long row of tall arched windows let sunshine into the room. I took a few steps, and the light fell on my shaved face.

Hundreds of courtiers packed the room. Their eyes fell on me—prying, gaping, gawking. To add to the discomfort this caused, the belt was squeezing me again. It wound up to my chest and my throat and tightened like a noose. I pulled at the neck of the tight silk tunic until a seam tore.

Pyttel nodded, urging me forward. I took a few more steps, and he followed. It was a long way to the dais where the King sat upon his throne. The crowd pressed in around me, smothering me. A drop of sweat ran down my temple, heat rushed through my veins. I stopped to wipe it and let my hair fall across my face. I longed for my wolf skin to cloak me. I wanted to run…needed to run…but I could not move.

Pyttel's hand touched my shoulder and urged me gently forward again. I tore off the silver fibula that clasped the heavy mantle around my shoulders. They both dropped to the ground. The rope around my chest loosened, and I took a deep breath.

Some of the courtiers gasped, and others smirked. I bared my teeth and glowered through the strands of hair on my face. They muttered and stepped farther away to let me through.

"Such behavior!"

"…a lowly tracker…"

"…a peasant…a wild man from the woods…"

Pyttel moved close to me and whispered, "Stop glaring. You are scaring them."

I fixed my gaze on the King's throne at the front of the hall. It was elevated by six steps on a dais in a large alcove. A domed ceiling crowned the throne alcove. A dozen heavily armed guards stood around the dais, and a hundred more were posted about the great hall. There was no cushion on the King's marble throne. His message was clear, "My place is hard, as is my justice."

A magnificent jeweled sword hung at the King's side, and his bright sapphire mantle spanned his broad shoulders. He held the Holy Spear in his right hand—his scepter.

I reached the steps to the dais, relieved to face away from most of the crowd. General Theoderic and Pepin, the King's hunchbacked son, stood near me. Pepin's young face shined, but General Theoderic's expression remained hard as a rock. The other magnates, two bishops, and members of the royal family all stood nearby.

Pyttel moved to my side and tucked his hands under his habit. He shifted nervously, like a teacher watching his pupil perform, then gave me a crooked wink.

A herald climbed the steps and addressed the crowd. An absolute silence settled over the hall.

"I present Tracker," said the Herald, "the savior of God's Holy Spear from the pagan Saxons."

"Come forward, Tracker," said the King.

I climbed the steps up the dais slowly. When I reached the top, the King rose. "Tracker, a simple huntsman from the south, has restored the Holy Spear and all its powers to me, ruler of Christendom, God's chosen King. You have earned God's blessing and my favor. As my reward for this great act of loyalty, I bestow upon you a place of honor in my court. From this day hence, you are to be known as the Royal Scout and Huntsman. Tracker, do you accept the honor and the duties of Royal Scout and Huntsman?"

I bowed my head stiffly, letting more hair fall into my face. "Yes, My King."

"I will accept your oath of fealty."

I hesitated.

*Your oath to the Christian King is what will make you a man among men, worthy of grace, one of God's flock.*

I knelt slowly and began the oath that Pyttel had taught me. "I, Tracker, make it known that I am the liege man of Karl the Great, King of the Franks." The words poured from my mouth, but I tried not to listen to them. "I will respond to the King's summons and aid him as called. I will remain loyal and do nothing to endanger the King, his family, his nobles, or his royal power. I will stay true to my bap...baptism..." I faltered but took a deep breath and finished. "...and keep faith with the Lord, Our God."

"Rise, Tracker, Royal Scout and Huntsman," the King said.

I stood, and he presented me with a sword and sheath. He embraced me and kissed my left cheek, then he smacked the side of my head. My ear rang from his blow.

"Tracker, Royal Scout and Huntsman, be acknowledged by my court," he said.

I had not held a sword before. I pulled it carefully from the sheath, feeling its weight and balance. It was light compared to my long axe, almost delicate. Its blade gleamed, made of the finest Frankish steel, worth the cost of an entire farm and a slave. Priceless, the mark of a noble Scola horseman. Was this a sign from my Heavenly Father? Would I feel God's grace now?

I turned to face the crowd, so many strangers gaping at me. I looked past them to the beaming face of Pyttel, alive with madness.

# What Most Men Would Give

~~~

The King left the hall escorted by his guards, leaving several at my side on the dais. As soon as he was gone, the hall filled with the chattering of hundreds of strange voices. The courtiers closed in on the dais, but the guards pushed past them and escorted me through the mass.

Pyttel was left to deal with questions from the curious courtiers. They swarmed around him, and his mouth dropped open.

The guards took me back to my quarters. The doors closed behind them, and the room was quiet. I was glad to be away from the crowd and ran to the window. I threw open the shutter, leaned out, and almost fell into the courtyard. This morning I owned two axes, a wolf skin, and a pair of threadbare breeches. Now I was draped in silk and held a fine Frankish sword—which I did not know how to wield.

I stripped off the layers, feeling a little better as each one dropped to the floor—silk tunic, linen shirt, and boots. I undid the straps tied around my feet and legs and let them fall with the breeches.

I threw on my wolf skin, picked up my axes, and leaned out the window again, breathing deeply. The air was cooling as the sun set, and servants began lighting torches in the courtyard. I could see over the wall into the town of Paderborn—dark and empty. Most were in the great hall.

"What are you *doing?*"

I had not heard Pyttel enter the room, and I wished he had stayed out.

"Breathing," I said.

He scanned me from head to toe. "And you say *I* am the mad one?" He was carrying the items I had dropped in the great hall. He gathered up my other clothes and tossed them all at me. "Get dressed! We have to be at the feast soon."

The clothing hit me and fell to the ground.

"I am not going," I said.

"You are a part of court now. You must."

I stared out the window. Beyond the walls of the palace and the town, the treetops swayed in the breeze.

*The forest awaits*
*…untamed*
*Where the Raven, the Eater of Souls, searches for prey*

*Return to the wilds*
*I hunger*

*Her eyes like fire*
*Beyond the walls*

But she did not appear here, in the King's palace where the sound of soldiers talking and laughing floated up from the courtyard.

I slammed the shutter closed and threw on the shirt and tunic. I groped at the mantle, unable to arrange it. Pyttel fussed with it until the folds draped properly across my shoulders and secured it with the fibula.

"Breeches." He grinned. "You have to wear breeches."

I groaned and pulled them on, then I wound the long linen strips up my feet and legs and put on the boots.

"You will get used to it," he said. "You have received a high honor from the King. That comes with a price."

"So he is no longer in my debt, but I in his."

He sighed and pulled a small dagger and sheath out from under his habit. The hilt sparkled with gems. "He has also given you something with which to cut your meat."

"What price for this?" I asked.

He grimaced and attached the sheathed dagger and sword to my belt. "Of course, you must wear the King's sword as well. What most men would give for such a sword! Now, let us enjoy the feast…and remember the rules I taught you."

# The Guest of Honor

The guards escorted us to the great hall, lit by torches and a large open fire in the center. Benches and long tables covered with white linen had been brought out and arranged around the fire. Courtiers filled every seat, drinking, talking, and laughing loudly. They hushed when I walked past.

The King's table presided over all at the front of the hall. The guards took me to the seat to his right. Queen Hildigard sat to his left. She held her head proudly, the honeyed woman who conceived the heirs of the King. I avoided her gaze. The royal children sat next to her. Pepin the Hunchback beamed at me.

The King stood, and the crowd followed suit. He lifted a large golden drinking horn and smiled.

"Welcome to my table Tracker, Royal Scout and Huntsman," he said then turned to address the crowd. "I sent for Tracker from the Alps mountains to hunt down the rebel

Widukind and learn the secrets of the Externsteine. He made great progress with this, and upon hearing of the theft of the Holy Spear, he hunted down and killed the thieves. To my great sadness, they were men on whom I had bestowed high trust and honor; traitors who betrayed their King and their God.

"When Tracker retrieved the Holy Spear, he could have heeded the Devil and kept it for himself. My own Scola soldiers, men of greater nobility, had turned away from honor and done so, but when this humble woodsman held the greatest relic in Christendom in his hands, he chose to return it."

The King lifted the drinking horn, longer than his arm. Gold and gemstones trimmed the lip, glimmering in the light. "A toast to Tracker, a heroic man of profound honor and faith who has returned the Holy Spear to me."

My cheeks flushed under the sight of every courtier in the room. They toasted, but few were smiling. Chamberlain Adalgis and Horse Master Gallo, seated at the nearest table, barely lifted their silver-rimmed horns. Count Hessi, sitting farther away, scowled and did not toast.

The King drank deeply and offered his horn to me. It was the same creamy smooth beer I had tasted the night of the general assembly.

I thought of words Pyttel had taught me. "It is an honor to drink from your horn, My King," I said, wiping beer from my chin.

"The honor is mine," he replied.

Pyttel had not told me that the King would say this. Did he expect a certain response? I began to sweat. What to say? My tongue wedged itself in my mouth, but before I could say anything, he offered me the seat next to his and sat.

"I make all important toasts with good Frankish beer in a

drinking horn," he said. "It is a tradition that goes back many generations." He leaned close. "This beer is brewed only for me, deep in the forest by beautiful women with huge tits." He chuckled. "Actually, they are hags, but imagining the tits makes good beer taste better."

I made a small smile. When he saw it, he laughed heartily, and my grin widened. He drank and offered me the huge horn again. It shielded my face, but I could see beyond the tip of it.

General Theoderic was positioned closer to the King than Gallo and Adalgis. He was accompanied by his wife, a harsh looking woman who matched his austerity. He tipped his horn to me.

Gallo sat with a young woman of about fifteen. She wore her hair loosely—probably his unmarried daughter. She gaped openly at me until Gallo jabbed her with his elbow.

Adalgis and Gallo whispered to each other, glancing at me. They sneered, and Adalgis sank his long pointy nose deep into his drinking horn.

The Saxon Count Hessi and his Frankish child bride were seated farther from the King's table than the Frankish lords. The girl kept her head lowered and her hands in her lap.

After we had emptied the horns, servants provided glass drinking vessels and flagons of wine. The glass was so delicate; I was afraid I would break it.

"Do you like my wine?" the King asked.

"…sweet," I said.

He squinted and clucked his tongue. "Yes, too sweet, but the women—and God—prefer it to beer." He nodded toward a table of young women. They blushed and giggled when they saw us looking at them.

"They are all anxious to hear more about you," he said. "I

daresay you will have your pick of any of them but be prudent about it. Do not sully the virgin daughters of the nobles. Take my word." He rolled his eyes. "It causes more trouble than it is worth….and over there…" He gestured to another table where several bejeweled women sat with their children. "Those are my concubines. I assume you are clever enough to stay away from them."

I nodded.

"The wisest choice for you is simplicity—visit the brothel outside the town walls. The best girls are reserved for my court. Pick a few favorites if you want, and I will have them kept for you." He finished his glass of wine. "That should keep you entertained until you marry."

Marry? My jaw dropped, but before I could say anything, the food was served.

The King licked his lips "We had a good hunt, and there is a lot of meat. Soon you will ride and hunt with me too. With your tracking skills and my keen instinct, we will bag some big game together. I will take you to forests far away from these bedeviled wilds—my private forest full of boar, bear, and bull aurochs with magnificent trophy horns."

The hunt! Far from the forest of the Raven and her standing stones! I forgot all thoughts of marriage and found an easy smile. "I look forward to it, My King." The words flowed from my mouth.

He winked. "I am as anxious to get away from court and these cursed heathen lands as you are." He raised his wine glass enthusiastically. "To our first hunt!"

I toasted and wondered if this was how God's blessing felt. I saw Pyttel with Alcuin and the other scholars at the table next to the General's. Pyttel nodded, and I grinned.

Two servants carried an entire roasted venison through the hall. They grunted, heaving it onto our table, which shuddered under the weight of it.

The golden brown skin glistened, and the smell of roasted fat filled the hall. I was not hungry, but my mouth still watered at the rich aroma. The King drew a jeweled dagger and carved the first haunch, then he set it on my plate.

"Thank you, My King." The words rolled off my tongue more easily now. Maybe our shared love of hunting had helped, or perhaps the beer and the smell of meat were making me more agreeable.

The King and the entire court waited until I took the first bite. The haunch was five times the size of my plate, and I used both hands to lift it to my mouth. I bit through crisp, buttery skin and into tender meat that melted on my tongue. The juices ran down my chin. I grinned at the King and wiped them away.

"That will fatten you up in a hurry!" The King slapped me on the back, and some in the court laughed.

Servants swarmed through the hall serving more platters of food. A band of musicians began playing. A player blew a flute. Another strummed a lyre, and a drummer struck a beat. The court chattered merrily, but I sensed a tension in the air. They were not as merry as they appeared.

I tore at the haunch and ate until my stomach felt like it would burst. The music stopped, and the room fell quiet. I glanced at the crowd through the strands of hair that lay over my face. All eyes had fallen upon me. The courtiers wrinkled their noses and curled their upper lips. They smirked and glared boldly…prying, gaping, gawking.

The belt tightened around my bloated stomach. I wanted to tear off the layers of clothes, cloak myself in the wolf skin, and pull the mask over my face.

I dropped the haunch, and it crashed onto the plate. Wiping the grease from my beard with my sleeve, I glowered at them until I noticed Pyttel. He was shaking his head frantically.

*Do not cast your demon eyes*
*Guest of honor*

I gulped from my wine glass.

"Music!" the King ordered.

The musicians began playing again, and the courtiers returned to chatting, peering at me over their wine glasses. I tipped back my glass and saw their distorted faces through the red wine. It warmed my stomach, and every time I emptied my glass, a servant refilled it.

More roasted meat was set before me—boar's head, pork, chicken, and goose. Pheasant and swan were served dressed in their feathers. I pulled out the dagger and cut small pieces of meat. The King nodded in approval as I picked at the food, eating with the thumb and middle finger.

Horse Master Gallo ate like a sow at a trough, following few of the rules Pyttel had taught me. He sneered at me as he stabbed his meat with a dagger. He gnawed on bones, spat, and picked gristle from his teeth, wanting me to know exactly what he thought of me. His daughter cast bold looks at me when he looked the other way.

The food and wine flowed onto the table all night. Bread dripped with melting butter and sticky honey. Bowls were packed with spiced legumes and carrots, eggs, cheese, and baked apple tarts. I drank and ate until I thought I would burst and tasted countless flavors that were new to me.

"I have not eaten such food before," I said to the King.

"Spices! Pepper, cumin, and cloves," the King said. "Merchants from the east bring them at great cost, but they are worth it. My favorite is the cinnamon that flavors the apple tarts." He took a bite of a tart and sighed with delight. "As sweet and tangy as my favorite redheaded concubine."

I tasted a tart—sticky and warm—and understood what he meant.

*Sweet musk and hawthorn*

"I have no taste for bland women or bland milk curds and broth," the King said, emptying his wine glass. "Now that everyone is in good humor, I have several things to discuss with you. I am moving east to Francia soon with most of the court. I cannot stay here any longer to deal with the Saxons. There are many demands to address and threats to quell on the far fringes of my kingdom. You, however, will remain here with General Theoderic."

"I want to stay with you, My King," I lied. I wanted to escape, far away from the perfumed palace and the Raven's haunt. Far away from all of it.

The King grinned. "I would love to keep you at my side, but I need you here for now. You will stay in Saxony."

My head was beginning to spin. "What of the hunt—your private hunting grounds?"

"The greatest priority now is to carve a clear road through the Teutoburg Forest and route out Widukind and his Wulfhednar. You will advise and assist General Theoderic in suppressing Saxon unrest as he sees fit. You will scout the route for the Hellweg to the Externsteine, keep watch to protect the workers, and collect information about the movements of Widukind and the rebels. If all goes well this summer, we will rendezvous in late fall for hunting—after Widukind is caught."

My face fell. "Yes…My King," I mumbled, finding it difficult to swallow the last drops of wine.

*Blood of Christ*
*Dripping from the crown of thorns*
*From hands impaled by iron nails*
*Ribs pierced by the Holy Spear*
*Endure…*

*Submit to the Lord*
*Submit to your king*
*Fight for your soul*

"General Theoderic has spoken highly of you," said the King. "He is my best general for good reason. His assessment of his men is impeccable, but do not expect him to show his favor openly. You will have to earn what esteem you get from him."

"Yes, My King."

"And remember the story I have told about you, *Tracker*. No one is to know anything of Gerwulf."

A lump formed in my throat…his story was both a fallacy and a truth I could not deny.

# Grace

The next morning, guards escorted Pyttel and me through the palace to the King's chapel. I was a guest of the King, not his prisoner, yet somehow I felt so.

It would be the first time I attended mass since my excommunication. My heart beat faster with every step through the endless halls. My sight was bleary, and my head pounded from the wine I drank the night before.

What awaited me in the House of the Lord? Would He embrace me or strike me down? For a moment, I hoped we would get lost in the huge palace.

"Stop fretting and have faith." Pyttel touched my arm. "You have won your soul. Do not fear." His eyes danced. "Faith."

I gripped my cross, and it reassured me—until we descended a staircase and stepped into the courtyard where the nobles and the King's household were gathering. They were all there—Count Hessi, Horse Master Gallo, Chamberlain Adalgis, and General Theoderic.

Hessi pulled his rich mantle close, as if trying to shelter himself from me. Gallo glared and spat through his missing teeth. He whispered something to Adalgis. General Theoderic looked past me with stone-like eyes, then all of them followed us to the chapel. The doors opened…

I was blinded by light.

*Glorious light*
*Alive with color*
*The color of heaven and Christ's blood*
*Bloody red cross…anguished*
*Blue Paradise shining above*

The bell tolled, and the monks chanted, their voices deep and sorrowful. They mourned the death of the Son of God with long, ringing echoes.

*The walls, the floor pulsing with His agony*
*The rumbling of God, the Father*

*Surrounded by saints*
*Light haloing their blessed heads*
*Heads without ears and noses*
*Fingerless hands praying*
*Pieces of flesh I coveted*

*Yet, Mary, Mother of Christ*
*Stands whole in golden light*
*Honeyed woman*
*Holy Spirit in her palm*
*All that is good and pure*

*All that is right*

*Grace*

I was overwhelmed with the vision and fell to my hands and knees in the chapel doorway. "Hail Mary, full of grace…" I whispered, my voice trembling. "…the Lord is with thee. Blessed art thou among women, and blessed is the fruit of thy womb."

God's light streamed through a colored glass window above the altar. Hundreds of bits of glass fit together to make the bloodied cross and blue sky. The walls were painted with pictures of the saints, their bodies now whole—and Mary was gone.

The Bishop and the King, Holy Spear in hand, stood in the front of the chapel. Pyttel knelt next to me, and the King and the rest followed. They recited the prayer.

My lips moved, but the words were lost.

*She is gone.*

Mass passed in a haze of pungent incense, filling the chapel, rising heavenward. The Latin prayers I understood, but they had no meaning, and the sermon was lost to me. My hands went cold, clasped tightly around my cross.

*Mary is gone.*
*Mother is gone.*

# Only God Needs to Know

After mass, I was called to a meeting with the King. I welcomed the diversion and pushed the Mass from my mind as I approached the private audience room. Heavy doors fortified with iron barred the entrance and creaked loudly on stout hinges as they opened.

King Karl and General Theoderic looked up from the table strewn with maps and documents. They frowned, furrowing the rolls on the back of the General's neck.

Did they want to speak of my prostrating myself in Mass?

"My King." I bowed.

"Tracker, there is much to discuss before I leave," he said. "As I mentioned last night, matters demand my attention elsewhere. I will be leaving Paderborn tomorrow."

I was relieved that he did not mention Mass.

He nodded toward the General. "General Theoderic will take command here for the summer. You will move to quarters adjoining his and serve him as his personal guard. You will also work as his scout and provide counsel on tracking and ambush tactics."

The General cleared his throat. "You have more tactical knowledge of the Teutoburg Forest and the Wulfhednar than anyone else," he said. "You are the only Christian in the kingdom who knows how to find the Externsteine. I want your expertise to extend the Hellweg to the Externsteine and to plan an invasion to take their stronghold."

The King crossed his stout arms. "I had tasked the Saxon Count Sidag with extending the road, but since he deserted, his peasants have stopped working," he said. "They are likely rebel supporters or rebels themselves. General Theoderic has taken control of Sidag's lands in Westphalia, and I have designated extra troops to ensure the peasants remain under tight control and work to clear the road. I have also assigned Horse Master Gallo to Paderborn for the season. He will train more noble youths as horsemen to build my forces on the Saxon borderlands."

"It is crucial that these preparations are completed this summer," said the General. "I suspect Widukind has far more followers than we thought. The attack must occur as soon as possible before he can rally more rebels. The work will begin tomorrow."

"So soon?" I said. "What plans have been made?"

"The road between here and the Lippespringe garrison is well-worn and relatively secure." Theoderic traced the road on one of the maps with his finger. "It must be widened, though. The work begins immediately with local Frankish workers from Paderborn. Beyond Lippespringe, the road becomes overgrown and disappears in the forest. My soldiers will begin rounding up Sidag's peasants and bringing them here to work on it. During that time, I will make plans to cut deep into the forest." He paused. "Can you read maps, Tracker?"

"Some."

He pointed to a large area northeast of Lippespringe on the map. "I believe the Externsteine lies somewhere in this area, but I must map its exact location and the most feasible route for building the road."

I studied the map. The areas firmly under Frankish control were well detailed, including the location of Paderborn, the Lippe River, and Lippespringe, but most of the Teutoburg Forest remained blank.

"The Raven's Stones are here," I pointed to the site, "and there is a rebel Saxon village nearby, here. The villagers, free and half-free, have sided with Widukind and have harbored him as well."

"Are you sure about this?" asked Theoderic. "Those farmers own some of the most fertile and fruitful lands in Saxony. They would risk losing much if they rebel."

"I have had no trouble from them in the past," the King said. "They remained loyal to me when other nearby villages rebelled several years ago. Their priest reports that they are good Christians, attending mass and remaining faithful."

"I know what I saw and heard. *Fallaces sunt rerum species.*"

"Yes, appearances are deceptive," the King said. "You have mentioned that before. You were correct then…"

General Theoderic raised his brows subtly at my Latin. "My King, if you are confident of this, I will mount an immediate attack on the village as an example to others," he said. "It has no defenses and can be razed by a small retinue of horsemen long before the Hellweg is finished."

The King smoothed his moustache. "No. We will wait. Widukind will likely return there if he thinks it is safe, and Tracker may learn more of the rebellion by observing their activities. I can also collect my full tax from their stock and crops before the army invades and takes everything as plunder. Until then, the roadwork must continue with utmost haste. Hack, burn, destroy any obstacles or anyone who interferes." The King's eyes blazed into mine. "Use any means necessary."

I read his meaning clear enough.

*Do what you must, Wulfhedinn.*
*Some things only God needs to know.*

# Farewell the King

That afternoon, I moved into a room adjoining General Theoderic's quarters. Pyttel met me in the quarters we had shared as I gathered my few belongings.

He was beaming. "I could hardly wait to talk to you after Mass! What happened? Did you hear the voice of God? Did the Holy Spirit descend upon you?"

"Yes…" And *no.*

His face beamed. "Yes! Yes! I felt it too." He clapped me in an embrace, laughing. "You have done it…saved us both. I know it. I hear God now, telling me…now in my ear." He pointed frantically. "I feel it! Right here!"

"Yes," I repeated.

"My killing time…it is all over now."

I envied him. His soul was as light as if he was hearing the songs of angels, and he probably was. I envied him.

In the morning, I joined General Theoderic, Pyttel, and

Horse Master Gallo in the courtyard to bid farewell to the King. Holy Spear in hand, he leapt on the back of his magnificent steed like a man half his age. Queen Hildigard reined next to him, and Prince Pepin and the older children filed in just behind. A cart with the youngest followed.

The King and Queen led the family procession out of the palace, escorted by the king's personal guards outfitted in matching mail armor. Chamberlain Adalgis rode next with more guards, the royal baggage train, and the rest of the court. The ranks of cavalry and foot soldiers brought up the rear guard.

Count Hessi was also leaving with his Frankish child-bride. His bulk of flesh required mounting steps to climb onto his mount. The girl's bottom lip quivered, and she wiped a single tear from her cheek.

Pyttel put this hand over mine. "I hate that Saxon bastard too," he whispered. "He is hardly the Christian he pretends to be, but wait. He will get his just deserts. God has told me this."

I nodded as their dust settled in the courtyard.

Theoderic turned to me. "The work on the Hellweg has begun. Some of the workers have started earlier, and you will begin regular patrols around the area."

Within an hour, we rode from the palace. I wore my wolf skin and my old breeches, feeling much better in them. I carried my long axe, keeping my francisca in my old belt. I had almost left behind the fine new dagger and sword from the King but thought the better of it. They hung heavily on my waist, but iron was as light as air compared to the weight of court clothing.

The General dipped his chin slightly, eying the weapons and skin. "Good; you will need them all," he said.

I was sure now that he knew I was Wulfhedinn—and he seemed glad of it.

We rode through Paderborn and out the gates. The scent of the perfumed palace faded behind me. We spurred our horses and covered the five miles to Lippespringe at a trot. I was glad the road did not pass close to Wodan's Spring.

We soon came to the walls that surrounded the general assembly grounds. Beyond there the road narrowed and disappeared into the brush. The area was crowded with soldiers and workers. Sweat glistened on the backs of men who chopped and hacked at the dense underbrush. Other men dug a ditch to drain a swampy area, using the dirt to fill and level the road. They must have started working well before dawn as they had already cut a large swath through the forest. I was impressed with how fast the General had organized and launched the road project.

Pyttel was walking up and down the line with two priests. They blessed every worker and section of the road. He winked and continued his work.

"Every able-bodied Frankish freeman of Paderborn is working on the road here," the General said. "A contingent of soldiers is rounding up the local Saxon peasants. I expect them to start arriving tomorrow. I have also sent dispatches farther afield to summon more soldiers and peasants from my estates in the Rhineland. It will be at least a week before they start arriving, but much can be done in the meantime with the resources at hand."

He reined to a stop. "The soldiers will stay close to the work area to protect it from ambush. You will scout a wider range of the forest, day and night, for any signs of the rebels. Keep a close watch on the Externsteine and the rebel Saxon village, and report immediately to me with any new activity there. You will also move ahead of the project and survey the best route to cut the road."

I nodded, wishing I could have left with the King, far from the palace, the Teutoburg Forest, and the Raven's Stones.

"Kill any Saxon lurking in the woods near the road without purpose," he said. "If you have the opportunity to take Widukind, do so—I do not care how."

*Do what you must, Wulfhedinn.*
*Some things only God needs to know.*

"Go now," he said, "and do not show yourself at the palace unless you have something to report. It is no place for you."

I swung my leg over my mount and slid to the ground.

"What are you doing?" he asked impatiently.

I handed him my reins. "What I must."

I went to Pyttel's side and knelt, folding my hands. "Bless me Brother, before I enter the forest."

"Of course," he said. "God be with you and protect you on your mission into the pagan wilds. In the name of the Father, the Son, and the Holy Spirit." He made the sign of the cross over me and kissed me on the cheek. "Remember that you are no longer Gerwulf the Wulfhedinn," he whispered. "Fight for your soul, Tracker, fight."

I rose and disappeared into the forest. The ground was soft under my feet as I pulled up the wolf hood. Leaves rippled in the breeze. I stopped, sure that the Raven, the Eater of Souls, was lying in wait.

I scanned the forest and the sky and lowered my ear to the ground. There was no sign of her; not her black wing, nor the scent of sweet musk and hawthorn. Still I decided to venture no further from the road. I stayed low behind the vegetation, rising up just enough to peer at the workers. I would patrol farther afield tomorrow.

At dusk, work stopped, and they all made camp within the abandoned walls of the Lippespringe garrison. They lit fires, cooked, and drank. I snuck through the escape hole and found a dark corner where I burrowed into the ground and curled up, listening to their voices until I fell asleep.

I returned to the forest long before dawn. The moon shone brightly, casting no shadow but my own. I kept one eye on the sky and the other on the woods around me, but saw no sign of the Raven or the shield maiden. I walked farther from the road, slowly and tentatively.

Something shuffled in the brush behind me. Drawing my axes, I turned and nearly tripped over a tiny fawn. It lifted its head and took an unsteady step, trembling on gangly legs, then bounded off.

How had I not heard a clumsy little fawn before it was underfoot? Why had I not smelled it? Its mother must be close, but I did not sense her either.

I broke out in a cold sweat, and my heart pounded. Widukind's Wulfhednar could have surrounded me, and I might not have known it. The wolf skin lay cold on my back, giving me neither warmth nor the senses I used to have. Was it a sign of God's grace as Pyttel had said? I held my cross, but it gave me no comfort either.

I ran back to the road and stayed close to it, watching the Saxon workers from the trees. The workers dragged their feet and grumbled about being forced away from their fields and livestock. When the guards turned their backs, they spat and stopped working altogether. They kept their tools tightly in hand, glaring at the soldiers. I decided to stay close in case they rebelled. I would patrol farther afield tomorrow.

I spent the night inside the garrison wall and found a reason to stay near the road the next morning—and for several mornings after. The Saxons had made their resentment clear, but they made no attempt to rebel or attack the soldiers. It was quiet, almost too quiet, so I stayed close. I would patrol tomorrow.

A few more days passed as more soldiers and workers poured into Lippespringe from the General's Rhineland estates. The stink of the midden piles was growing as rapidly as my beard. I had been gone long enough. It was past time to report to General Theoderic, but I had not accomplished anything he had ordered—not patrolled widely, nor spied on the rebel Saxon village, nor surveyed the best route to cut the road.

I scratched the scruff on my face, dreaded shaving it, and headed back toward the palace having no idea what to tell him.

# Taste the Beast

~~~~~

Icame to the walls of Paderborn as the sun was setting. It shaded a cluster of cottages outside town. Four Scola horsemen rode up from town and dismounted outside one of them. They tied their mounts, staggering and talking loudly, then disappeared inside.

All of the shutters were closed tightly except one, hanging askew from a broken hinge. Drunken laughter poured out from the gap. It drew me to the window, and I hovered near it, hearing voices of men and women.

A young woman appeared from around the corner like a ghost. She stared at me with wide eyes.

"Do you want to come in?" she asked.

"…uh…no…" I pulled my skin around me and began to walk away.

"You are Tracker, the new Royal Huntsman?" she asked after me.

I stopped. "Yes."

"We have been waiting for you. The King says we are to take good care of you. Come inside." Her hand touched my shoulder.

"I...must report to the General."

She walked around me blocking my path. "We have heard much about you...a common huntsman who returned the Holy Spear to the King. You are his new favorite." She came closer. "What does it feel like?"

She moved so near that I could feel her breath and smell the perfume she rubbed between her breasts. She ran her fingers through the fur of the skin.

I stepped back.

"Ah...you are shy." She pressed against me and put her other hand over mine. "So charming in one so big and strong, who is honored by the King." She drew her body against me. "We do not have to go inside with the others," she whispered.

Her scent mixed with mine. She wrapped her leg around mine and pulled the wolf skin open, running her hands over my chest. "I feel God beating inside you. Let me lie with you and press my heart on yours."

She stood on her toes, pushing her breasts against me and lifted her lips to mine. I turned away, so she dropped to her knees as if praying. She unbuckled my belt, pulled down my breeches and lowered her head. Her wet lips fell over my cock in a manner that could not be denied by any man, and I gave in to her. When it was over, I shivered, my blood running cold. She pressed next to me, her body like ice.

"You are like a wolf," she said. "I can taste the beast in you."

A raven flew down and perched above us—merely a black bird roosting for the night. I pushed the whore away and fled into town.

I ran to my chamber and bathed, rubbing my skin with a brush until it was raw. I shaved, running the razor roughly over my face until it bled, then dressed in the silk tunic.

I reported to General Theoderic. He sat at a table surrounded by a mountain of dispatches and documents, stacked as high as his rutted brow. He did not look up from writing. "I thought the woods had swallowed you up," he said.

"There has been nothing to report."

He set his quill in the inkpot and frowned. "What have you done to your face?"

I touched my chin, feeling the dried blood. "I shaved."

"Did you use a sword? You're a bloody mess. For the sake of heaven, have the grooms shave you." He shoved a stack of documents to the side. "Now, what have you to report?"

"The forest remains quiet," I said. "I have seen no trace of rebels or of Widukind."

*Or the Eater of Souls*

"What of the activity at the rebel village?"

"I have heard no more talk of Widukind and the rebellion."

"…and the Externsteine?"

"It appears abandoned at this time."

He stood and clasped his hands behind his back and appraised me closely. It was easier to lie than I thought, but I was not sure if he believed me.

He began pacing. "The influx of Frankish soldiers may have intimidated Widukind. More likely, he is biding his time, waiting to strike when we let down our guard." He stopped. "You are to keep up your patrols, but tomorrow you will guide the road builders deeper into the forest. Have you marked the route?"

"Yes," I lied again.

"Good. Keep watch on the village and the Externsteine and let me know of anything you hear or see."

"Yes, My Lord." I bowed and returned to my chamber.

I tore off the tunic and dropped it in two pieces. I left the palace with my skin and weapons, having no intention of returning to the rebel village or the Raven's Stones.

# To Appease the Gods

————∿∿————

I bolted through town and out the gates onto the Hellweg. I could keep close to the road and continue to fool General Theoderic. I could for a while...

The road remained clear as I ran to the Lippespringe garrison. At the wall, a breeze kicked up, carrying the smell of incense, stale beer, and goat's blood. A stout figure broke from the trees onto the road ahead. His bare white skin glowed, his hair dripping wet, and he carried a bloody basket—Pyttel... sacrificing at Wodan's Spring again.

"Monk," I called.

He startled and dropped the basket when he saw me. "Gerwulf! I mean Tracker! Praise God! Where have you been?"

"Tracking."

"I was afraid that you had deserted or that she had...did you see her...the Corpse Eater?"

"No."

"Hallelujah!" He held his arms wide and threw them around me. "Truly, we have been redeemed."

I pulled away. "Get dressed!"

"Yes, yes." He threw his habit over his head. "I have prayed for you Gerwulf, night and day, but God told me...in here," he tilted his head and pointed to his ear, "that you were on your own in the pagan woods. I was afraid for you...to appease the gods, I sacrificed..."

"I know."

"What happened to your face?"

"Nothing."

"What have you found? Are the rebels nearby?"

"I have seen no sign of them," I said.

He cocked his head, his eyes probing me. "No? Something is wrong. What is it? Did you see the Eater of Souls again?"

"No!"

"This is good, very good...and Widukind is staying quiet for now. Have you reported this to General Theoderic yet? He was here yesterday looking for you."

"I have seen him. He has ordered me to guide the road builders deeper into the forest in the morning. Tonight, I continue patrolling."

"Then I shall see you tomorrow. I will be there to bless the next section of the road. The closer they get to the Raven's Stones, the more they need my prayers." He put his hand on my shoulder. "Be extra careful and hold your cross and your faith tightly. Tonight is Hexennacht, Witches' Night. You should be in church, praying for protection with the rest of us until dawn, but I know you will refuse.

"I will not hide in a church," I said. "I fight for my soul."

He cackled. "And you have already won it," he said. "Still,

I will speak well of you to God and ensure He stays with you."

"Thank you, Brother," I smiled.

He grinned and winked. "Your smile is getting better. Soon, you may be truly happy."

I nodded and dodged into the woods, staying hidden until Pyttel was inside the wall. I was planning to sneak into the garrison to curl up in my corner for the night; sleep had come easily near the comforting voices of the workers and soldiers.

The breeze blew clouds over the moon, and it grew so dark that I lost sight of the road. Strange, I had only gone a few paces from it. It had to be close, a few footsteps. I retraced my steps but could not find it. It had vanished. I tried several directions, sure it could not be far. How could I have missed it?

*Wolf eyes falter*
*Every tree the same*
*Each fallen limb, stream, and rock…*
*Darkness, so much darkness*
*It must be near*
*She must be near*
*Unsure…my head spinning*

*I turn, and turn again*
*Walking in my own steps*
*Nothing familiar*
*…turn and turn again*
*I run blindly*

*The Raven calls*
*Screeching, cold ice down my neck*
*Stumbling*

*Dripping white flowers and sweet musk*
*…running, running*

*Rising in front of me*
*Giants looming overhead toward the moon*
*Luminous white stone, close enough to touch*
*…I reach…*

Something fell on me, tangling my limbs. I fought it, but the harder I fought, the tighter it ensnared me, a weighted mesh—a hunting net. My axes became tangled in it, so I reached for the dagger in my belt and grasped the pommel. Inching my fingers down onto the handle, I pulled it and slashed. My arms were free…a shadow jumped at me…

*A wolf face*
*Fangs snap*
*I slashed, hitting flesh*
*More wolves*
*Screaming, howling for my blood*
*I am hit, again and again*
*I fight and slash…*
*Harder blows at my face*
*I fall, my head spinning*
*Fangs tear into my arm and legs*
*…fight and slash*
*Iron and fangs rip through flesh*
*…then blackness*

# Carried on Raven's Wing

I shivered violently. My body shook in wet waves of burning heat, yet I was cold, icy cold. Murky shapeless forms floated around me. I smelled vague scents, familiar, yet strange. I tried to move beyond the shivering but was tightly encased in cold hard stone. It fit tightly around me, holding me in place on my back.

*Trapped*

I shivered in the stone hole, a long, endless time—or a brief moment.

Above me, a faint light flickered. Had it just appeared? It grew brighter until I could see stone above me, like a cave. I tried to move but was stuck in the hole.

A shadow appeared overhead—the wings and beak of the Raven.

*I hunger*

The Raven tore the cross from my neck and flung it aside.

*Feed the wolf*
*Feed the Raven*
*Fill me with your blood*

Her beak attacked, running through me, poking, stabbing over and over, like a needle jabbing deeply into my gut. I lay helpless, taking her punishment. She fed off my face, arm, and legs. Poking, stabbing, jabbing. Her eyes glowed red hot as a blacksmith's iron. They burned and seared my belly...stink of my own burning flesh.

I tried to scream. Moments later, a shriek echoed off the stone ceiling. Had it come from me? My body seized, but my mind was detached, beyond feeling. I struggled again...exhausted, drifting away, leaving my body inside the rock, floating into oblivion.

I was rising, out of the hole in the stone. I was gone, but my body lay in the hole, skin bloodied and seared...

*Was this death?*
*Was I being made a sacrifice?*

Something was near me. Spirit or creature of flesh? It had picked me up and carried me, soaring on waves of air, reaching higher into the heavens until it separated from me. I glided a while and then was falling...falling, tumbling into a scorching chasm. I fell into the fires of a burning village, choking on thick smoke. Gasping, choking.

Bodies of slain women and children littered the ground. I ran, tripping in the haze over the dead. Bloodied and mutilated, heads cut off, piled like rubbish at my feet. Nearest to me was the head and body of a woman, her face obscured by her long honey-colored hair.

The wind picked up and blew the hair off her face, one tendril at a time. The cheek, the jaw...a face I knew, buried a long time age.

*Run...run*

Something held me in place, kept me from moving or looking away.

*Run...run away*

I closed my eyes, but it was too late.

*Mother*

I choked. She was with me. I reached to touch her, blue pallor and ice. Brushing aside the last piece of her hair, I cradled her head, wishing desperately to feel life in her. She gaped at me. My heart pounded...my breath stolen.

Her body lay nearby, naked, bloodied, and bruised. A figure stood over, a beast on two legs, wolf's head and man's body.

*Wulfhedinn*
*Me*
*Father*

Time passed—or none at all. I was inside the cold tomb again.

*Drums beat*
*Heart pounding*

Sight returned slowly, faint and dim, subtle light near me...a torch. Figures danced on the stone ceiling above me, the shapes of wolves that moved on two legs, like men who were beasts—or beasts who were men.

*Drums beat*
*Heart pounding*

They danced, sometimes upright, sometimes like animals. Their dance carried me up and out of the tomb, past giant white stones. Torchlight flickered. Strange creatures came alive in the white stones, beasts with fangs, dragons that breathed fire...a dead man hanging from a tree from his arms. He had no face. He had the face of God.

*Drums beating...drums beating...*
*Pounding to the rhythm of my heart*

I rode on the back of the wolf to a staircase carved into stone, floating up the stairs, carried on the Raven's wing. We wound up and around the side of the huge rock until high above the trees. The full moon shone, almost within reach. I passed through a threshold, a gate—then it shut and locked. I was left in darkness.

*Drums beat*
*Heart pounding*

I was shivering again, laying somewhere between wakeful-ness and sleep, where I trembled until dawn.

# The Chamber of Stone

⁂

**B**irds were singing, hundreds of songbirds. Their song called me to awaken. Lost…unsure of up and down, as if floating in water. Water was all around me, yet my throat was parched.

*Water….*

The birdsong grew louder, and the water around me dissipated, leaving me dry.

*Water…*

My whole body ached and throbbed. Slowly one eye opened, but the other remained dark. Had it been blinded? I tried to touch it but could not move my hands.

A hazy glow came through a small round hole. It brought

meager light to me. My hazy sight cleared slowly until I could see part of my own swollen and bruised face. I could not open my jaw or breathe through my nose. I panted through my half-opened mouth, beaten and broken.

All around me was stone. I was lying in a chamber made of stone. It only had one opening, a small round hole to the clear blue sky.

Flashes of memory struck me—shivering helplessly in a cold stone hole, the tomb, *my* tomb? But this place was different...

Drums pounding. The Raven. The wolf. The burning village...where was I? I grasped for a piece of anything familiar but failed—pain and an overwhelming thirst pushing aside anything else.

*Water...*

Everything familiar was buried under an endless stretch of dry, cracked earth. I wanted to call out...I gasped air through parched lips, seeing dawn turn into day through the little hole in the stone wall.

I lay on a straw pallet, beaten and soaked with sweat and my own filth. I had been shivering violently, but it had stopped now, leaving me too weak to move. Taking a deep breath, I focused on moving my left hand. An agony shot up my arm, and I only managed to shift it slightly as it was tied down.

Gritting my teeth, I tried to move the other hand then my feet, but they were all bound tightly. I pulled feebly until I became dizzy and weakness overtook me.

I rested, gasping. It was a long time before the dizziness passed and I saw him—a man was standing at my feet.

I lifted my head, barely parting my cracked lips. My mouth was so dry I could scarcely whisper, "Water…"

He did not reply.

I gasped and dropped my head, unable to ask again.

The day outside the hole grew brighter, but the chamber remained dim. The man stood immovable all day. A guard and I was his prisoner, suffering thirst in darkness while the sun shone and birds sang outside.

A wolf howled a long haunting cry. It sounded distant, far outside the hole. When it stopped, silence remained. It called again, growing louder, stronger, and nearer until its cry echoed inside the stone walls.

The guard did not move.

The howling grew into snarling buried inside me, a familiar rage from the deep place where the beast dwelt.

I was Wulfhedinn, the cursed beast.

It burst with wrath and spite. I fought against the bonds on my wrists and ankles, but the struggle drained me. The beast could not overcome this. I tried to speak, to demand water and my release by the stone man, but I could only moan and try to catch my breath.

The guard did not move.

I was lost from everything except that which I wished to forget—the wolf and the Raven, the Eater of Souls. She had found me, sweeping in to perch on the edge of the hole.

"Let…me…go…"

My jaw and throat grated in agony. Had I spoken the words? Neither the Raven nor the guard responded. He stood like stone. I stared at him all day until he became clear—a face carved into the rock wall.

He had a knotted face, bulging eyes, and a wide mouth fixed

in a scream. It echoed across the stone walls, ringing in my ears. With my hands tied, I could not block the sound. It tormented me until my throat ached and burned...

The screams had come from me. Truly, I was in Hell, and my captor was the Devil.

Exhausted and abandoned, I could fight no longer and retreated into blackness.

# The Woman
# with the Caldron

⁘

Jawoke to bright, blinding light. I squinted, adjusting slowly to the glaring sun, glancing around. Someone had opened a timber door to my right and a window to my left. A warm breeze blew through the chamber. It carried out the stink of sweat and piss and brought in the smell of spring.

Spring. It was spring still, maybe early summer. Perhaps I had not lost too many days since coming here. I last remembered trees leafing, and flowers had been blooming...flowers that blossomed just before May Eve, Hexennacht—Witches' Night.

I had been deep in a forest—but where? What had I been doing? Where was I now?

The door and the window revealed nothing but blue sky as if I were perched in the heavens.

I closed my eye again, letting the sun warm me. When I opened it, a cloaked figure stood at the little round hole where the Raven again perched. Below the round hole was a stone pedestal carved into the rock, like a small altar. Runes were painted on the alcove walls around the altar. I tried to read them, but their meaning was beyond my grasp.

The figure's scent was familiar. It smelled of May flowers and a woman's body—sweet musk and hawthorn. I knew her, but from where? My memory was as beaten as my body.

The Raven hopped from the window onto the woman's arm. She stroked and whispered to it, a firm, yet soft voice. As if in response, the Raven flapped its wings and flew through the window.

*She sends the Raven....*
*How do I know her?*

My scrambled mind reached for memories that were too muddled to recall.

"You look better," she said. Her voice was strong, neither friendly nor hostile. I understood her words well enough but could not place the accent.

She turned, lowered her hood, and moved toward me.

I licked my cracked lips with a dry tongue. "Water...where?" I whispered, attempting to rise. Pain ripped through my gut and left arm and leg, and the bonds held tight.

"You are here with me now," she said. "I will give you everything you need."

"Let...me...go..." I struggled to speak louder, tugging weakly.

I gathered my energy and flailed. She set down a small caldron and placed a hand on my throat, pinching my windpipe, stopping me with two fingers.

"You will start bleeding again if you move too much." She glowered, her blue eyes like ice. "You are Wulfhedinn, but you are not immortal. Your blood will drain from you as fast as it drains from any man."

I nodded, and she released my throat. Her mantle fell open, revealing a sword sheathed at her side, its horn pommel close to my reach.

She noticed. "You cannot take it from me," she said, "and it will be a long time before your wounds heal and you regain enough strength to break these straps. Until then, you may as well eat."

She scooped up some broth from the caldron and cradled my head with her other hand. She raised the spoon to my lips. It smelled of hot chicken, leeks, and salt. So tempting—too tempting, but I hesitated to take it.

"You will die soon if you do not quench your thirst, Wulf-hedinn." She tilted her head, staring into my eyes. "I know how you thirst. You have no choice but to trust me."

She saw my deepest weakness, and I hated it. I writhed and yanked, fighting the bonds—fighting her—but thirst overtook me, leaving me powerless.

My cracked lips parted. She let a few drops slide into my mouth, wonderfully warm and wet on my parched tongue. My throat ached for it but was too weak to swallow. I felt like a dying infant in its mother's arms.

She set down the spoon and stroked my throat gently, making it relax. The broth ran smoothly down, warming my stomach, giving me new life.

I submitted completely to her. "More…"

"Good." She nodded with approval. "The gods and goddesses favor you, Wulfhedinn. You have survived the Three Days Sleep. You are ready to heal."

*The Three Days Sleep…?*
*What …?*

Questions ran through my mind, but they faded behind my hunger for more of her broth.

"More…" I pleaded.

She continued spoon-feeding me tiny amounts and stroking my throat to help me swallow. Soon I was able to swallow by myself. My stomach filled slowly. I felt strong enough to lift my head but allowed her to continue cradling it.

Her expression remained serious, but a softness settled in her eyes, now as blue as the sky outside the hole. They reminded me of another's. She rocked me subtly, as if unintentionally— like my mother had when she cared for me.

*Is this why she is familiar?*

Completely helpless, I needed more. I opened my mouth after every spoonful, but she would not feed me any faster.

"More…now." My voice was a little stronger, my throat less parched.

"That is enough for now." She put down the spoon and Mama faded. "You must start slowly. There will be plenty more soon. Soon I will bring you barley, then meat."

I tried to move again, feeling more determined, but the surge of strength faded. A pleasant drowsiness ran through my body, along with a mild bitterness on my tongue.

"Rest now," she said. "Let the broth ease your suffering."

Soon I floated to a distant place, far from where I could feel anything bad. I drifted pleasantly wrapped in pleasure, neither asleep nor fully awake.

Her long black hair fell forward as she removed the fur that covered me. I was naked underneath, lying in my own filth. Slashes and large purple and green bruises covered my body. I was thin, and my ribs protruded through slackened skin. Bloody linen dressings swathed my belly, left leg, and arm—my stronger axe arm.

I slipped into a contented state, unaware. Time passed…I was moving. My arms and legs were bending and stretching, free of the restraints. I glimpsed her and fell into the void again, but she was there with me. I imagined how beautiful she might be if she smiled.

Her warm hands bent and shifted my limbs, rubbing them. She was washing me with a wet cloth, briskly yet gently—face, body, and cock. She put me into such a state that I was unable to move.

She turned me over and ran a gentle finger down the scars on my back. "You have been flogged—scourged deeply, many times." Her strong voice softened. "Old scars…from childhood. Who did this to you?"

"God," I grunted, trying to turn over, to hide it from her.

"Well, he will not hurt you here," she said, holding me firm-ly. "This is *my* domain."

She gently cleaned my rear and rolled me on my side. How strong she was to move me so easily. I smelled fresh linen be-neath me, warm from hanging in the sun.

I stirred again as she peeled the wet dressings away from the wounds. I felt a distant achiness, almost as if the wounds belonged to someone else. A gaping hole in my abdomen stretched from hip to hip. A yellowish ooze seeped from the wound. A thick ointment covered the exposed bands of muscle. On my arm and leg were long slashes closed with stitches, also covered with ointment. She washed the wounds gently with water.

"They are healing well now." Her words took a long time to reach me, echoing through a long cave. "This one had festered." She pointed to the large one on my belly. "I sealed it with the fire iron of Donar, the Thunder God. It will leave a large scar, but with his blessing, you will live all the same. You are fortunate that our swords did not cut any deeper." She touched my blinded eye softly. "It too will improve, and your sight will return. It was difficult for us to take you down; it took a full dozen Wulfhednar." She left my side and walked toward the door. "But if you survived such whippings as a child, you will survive this and become all the stronger."

She had thrown so many words at me...what did she mean?

Again she was familiar, at the same time, a stranger. I wanted her to stay. I feared she would bar the window and the door and leave me tied in the dark with the stone man and the Raven.

I wanted her to return to my side, to feel her touch again, for her to care for my broken body and cradle my head in her arms. I craved the taste of her magical broth. It dulled the pain of my wounds, those that were new, and all that I had ever suffered. I needed it...I needed her.

I tried to call to her but could only mumble. The words in my thoughts got lost before reaching my tongue.

A large spider was spinning its web which reached across the sunny threshold. She scooped it up and set it gently on a crook in the wall. She carefully removed the web and mixed it into a jar of ointment.

I tried to reach into her eyes, to tell her to stay with me and never close the door.

She returned my gaze, stroking the hair off my forehead. Her fingers lingered there then she resumed her work.

She applied more ointment to all the wounds and covered them with fresh linen. She buckled the straps holding my wrists and ankles and covered me again with the fur. My stomach was full, my mouth moistened, and contentment overtook me.

"You will fall into a deep sleep soon. I will be back when you awake."

# I Have a Name

―――――～～～―――――

I roused as if no time had passed, time lost. The Raven and the stone man stood guard over me. The door and window stood open, but the sun now shone through the arched window instead of the door. It must have been late afternoon.

The fog in my head cleared slowly. I pulled at the tethers on my wrists and ankles, feeling a little stronger, but the bonds were stronger. My body ached and throbbed, and I thought of the nourishing broth and the woman with the caldron who fed it to me. She had promised to return.

A moment later she appeared, emerging from the blue sky through the open door. She carried a steaming caldron and a basket on her back. My mouth watered for her broth, and I longed to break free and grab the pot and devour its contents all at once.

"You are stronger," she said, "but you have a long way to go before you can break loose."

"Let me go!" I thrashed and tried to sit up.

Fighting triggered more pain, but I gritted my teeth and fought it. I would break away from her and her Raven, the stone man, and this place. I was strong now. I was Wulfhedinn.

"Where are my wolf skin and my cross?" I demanded.

"You have no need of a Christian cross. Your God has no power here." She put a strong hand on my chest and forced me down. "You will wear your wolf skin again when you are ready. Until then, I will hold your throat if I must."

Exhaustion overtook me, and I relented. My abdomen, arm, and leg throbbed. I panted, trying to hide the hurt and the fear that I had lost the cross—my God's cross, my mother's cross.

"You are in Wodan's land now," she said. "He will not forsake you as your God has done. Wodan rewards brave warriors. He does not punish them."

*Wodan? The Saxon War God*
*Saxony…the forest…the Teutoburg Forest*
*…I had been set against the Saxons, but by whom?*
*Why?*

"You will remember more as you heal and time passes," she said.

"You know that I am your enemy?"

"For now," she replied.

"Why do you keep me?"

"Because you are home now," she said.

*Home?*

She scooped broth from the caldron. "Eat. This will fatten you up. It is thickened with barley."

Her coddling confused and angered me. She tried to cradle my head, and I wrenched it out of her arms. "Give me my cross!"

She ignored me and lifted the spoon to my nose. I shook my head, but the aroma was overwhelming. My empty stomach growled, and my throbbing body ached for it. Reluctantly, I accepted—a small taste, no more.

The thick nourishing warmth slid down my throat. It had the same slightly acrid taste as the watery broth had, but it filled my churning stomach better.

"Good," she said.

I took another sip—a tiny bit more. That would be all.

It tasted better than the first, and I took more…and more. I ate as rapidly as she allowed. My mind raced with thoughts of breaking free of her when strong enough, but soon I returned to the place of pleasure. It robbed me of my will, and I allowed it, as much a prisoner of her soup as the ties on my wrists and ankles.

When my head whirled in soft delight, she untied me and moved and stretched all my joints. I tried to fight her, but I was sleepy—*so sleepy*. I drifted away…

And so it continued. The woman came several times a day with her magical soup—the witch. She appeared as I awoke and gave me the potion. After I was drowsy and helpless, she released and exercised my limbs. She collected more spider webs and cared for my wounds. The soup grew thicker, and soon she brought hearty stews made with carrots, cabbage, and meat. Every meal had the same bitter aftertaste.

As I grew stronger, I struggled harder between her visits, thrashing until beaten back by anguish and exhaustion.

And I continued to take her stew…knowing it weakened my resolve.

"Keep fighting, Wulfhedinn. It helps your muscles grow

strong," she said. "But do not think you can best me. All men fail, and by the time you are strong enough to challenge me, you will have become one with this place. You cannot escape it, our most sacred place. It is in your blood. Its roots grow back to the beginning of time. You are lodged in the greatest stone of them all—the great pillar that holds up the sky. Here you will recover your life and your spirit."

I did not understand; nor did I care. Instead, I planned for the time when I would be strong enough to take the sword from her. As the days passed, the swelling around my eye waned and vision slowly returned. I tried to keep my sights on her blade, forgetting my plans when she plied me with her magical stew.

One more day of the magical stew…one more…

Soon, I began to anticipate the stew more than fleeing. I drifted from meal to meal, day to night. How many days had passed? The time between her visits grew longer, and I grew more impatient for every feeding. One morning, my irritation exploded. She was late—very late, I was sure.

I twisted and tossed. "Where are you, witch?! Bring the stew!" My voice echoed off the stone walls, but she did not appear. I screamed again…and again…until there were no more words, only stridor and rasping for breath. The wolf's fury boiled my blood, and sweat ran down my body. I thrashed and growled, but the straps held.

All the while, the Raven sat on the little window, roosting comfortably. I bayed and writhed until I was exhausted and tears ran down my face. I gasped for breath, and the Raven cackled.

*Feast on the stew*
*…more…no more…more….*

*Feast, feast, feast*
*...more...no more...more...no more*

"Enough." I panted. "Enough..."

When she finally came, I refused her stew. "You are poisoning me, witch."

"Only a Christian would insult me so," she said slamming the lid on the caldron. "I use herbs blessed by the gods with healing properties. They help you rest and mend—until you need them no longer."

"I would rather feel everything than take any more of it. Bring me clean food."

"As you wish, Wulfhedinn."

"I have a name!" I snapped.

"Oh?" She raised a black brow. "And what would that be?"

"Tracker..." My voice trailed off. It was the first time I had heard it since coming here, and it sounded strange.

"Tracker?" she asked. "That is not a name. It is what you do. What is your real name?"

"Gerwulf."

The Raven squawked from her perch in the hole. She flapped her wings.

The witch smiled, lifting her round cheeks. "Yes, I know. It is good to hear you speak of it."

*She knows?*

"Who are *you*?" I asked, drawn into her eyes, familiar...from somewhere...

"I am no witch," she said, and the Raven screeched in the little window. "Soon enough, you will know who I am, Gerwulf."

# The Stone Tower

~~~

I lay awake after dusk. The Raven fluffed her feathers and settled for the night on the little window. Pain drew my attention away from her and the stone man. Without the potion, it was intense and impossible to sleep. My mind was clearer, but my body hungered for the bitter stew. One more bite could not hurt, and I would sleep, drawn into the place of pleasure again.

I clenched my jaw, tears rolled down my cheeks. My skin crawled with gooseflesh, and only the stew could stop it. I yearned for it…needed it so badly, it was nearly beyond bearing.

The Raven cackled. She and the witch knew I would relent and plead for more, beg like a helpless child.

I screamed in agony and frustration. I did not have the strength to refuse it, but the wolf did. I howled, feeling its power rise, fearsome enough to overcome anything. The wolf could deny the craving and see and think clearly. I howled again and began to take stock.

She had left me flat on my back. One arm was tied at my side and the other over my head. The straps were long enough to allow my arms to flex but too short to let me sit up.

The one on my upper wrist was a hand's breath from my mouth. I shifted toward it. I bit my tongue as a searing pain tore through my gut. I stopped until it subsided. I was so close; I almost tasted the leather. I tried again, digging my heels and my other hand into the pallet to push myself. I inched closer until I could crane my neck and reach it with my teeth.

This stretched my other limbs and pulled on the stitches. Breathing deeply, I relaxed for a moment then began to chew. I gnawed until my neck cramped and forced me to stop. I began again. Progress was slow, but the leather was softening. I was exhausted yet exhilarated by the thought of freedom. My jaw ached, and I rested until my energy returned. I would not concede to weakness. I would break free by daybreak.

The moon rose and lit the chamber in silver light. It streamed through the little window, glistening on the Raven's slick plumage. She shook her feathers and hopped from the window to the altar.

*She grows, lengthening upward, ripening*
*Curves of breast and hip shimmering in silver moonlight*
*Masked by the Raven*
*Floating to me, black feathers flying behind broad shoulders*
*Bare skin taut with strength*
*I know her*
*…sweet musk and strange flowers…*

*Bound and naked*
*Powerless against the smell of her body*
*She rises and mounts*

*…sweet musk and flowers I cannot place…*

*I seek her smell, yearn for it*
*Trace it into the past*

*The shield maiden spurs*
*Her pelvis tight against mine*
*Saddling, seizing me without granting release*
*Pulled through boundless depths*
*Riding hard*
*Galloping across ground and sky*

I gasped for breath. My heart pounded, and sweat covered my body. I tried to sit up but was held tight.

She was gone. The Raven perched, head under wing, in the round window.

What madness was this? A nightmare?

My heart would burst if it did not slow. Memories flooded my mind. I gasped for air.

…The witch with the caldron … she had chased me through the Teutoburg Forest. She was the shield maiden, the Raven spirit who rode with the rebel Saxon Widukind.

A warning…

*Never lose your cross…*

And I had lost it—to her, the Eater of Souls.

*The net falls*
*Snaring me*
*All is lost…*
*Motherless, Fatherless, Godless*

*Adrift...naked*
*The beast tears through my veins, my heart, my soul*
*Run...*

With new energy, I shimmied up the pallet toward the half-chewed tether on my wrist.

*Ripping, tearing*

The leather thinned, and finally, it snapped.

I reached to the other hand, unbuckled the strap, and pushed myself up. My stiff arms gave out, and my belly throbbed. I took several breaths, forcing my rigid joints and weak muscles to work. I sat up, panting and released my legs.

*Free!*

My excitement rose. She had left the timber door unbarred and open, and I had the whole night before she would return at daybreak. I rolled to the side of the straw pallet and attempted to stand, but everything moved slowly, painfully. I struggled until weakness and dizziness overtook me and fell back with a groan, rolling onto the stone floor.

The Raven tilted her head, watching me from the little window.

"You find this amusing?" I hissed.

She cackled.

I spat at her and looked for a way to support myself—the wall. I scooted there and pushed myself up, legs trembling. I leaned hard against the wall. My legs collapsed, and I fell again, frustrated and angry with my fragile state. If I did not muster the strength to get out the door, she would tie me up again when she found me. She had been right; I was too weak yet.

I rested then tried once more to stand. This time, I was able to steady myself. Hugging the wall, my feet shuffled toward the open door. My legs quivered. I stopped, breathing deeply—only a few more steps to go. Dawn would be coming soon, but if I could get to the door, I could get far enough into the forest to hide and rest.

I fell, whimpering. The Raven mimicked me with a shrill whining sound. I pawed at the ground and dragged myself slowly to the threshold. Reaching across it, I felt nothing but space below me—a doorway to nowhere.

I was higher than the treetops, swaying in the breeze, lit by the full moon. The chamber was atop a stone tower, the tallest of a line of giant white stones. It was so high that I felt closer to the stars than to the ground.

The witch had called it the greatest pillar of them all—the one that holds up the sky itself. I knew this place. I had been here before—the Externsteine. I was not in Hell; I was a living captive of the Raven's Stones.

The nearest pillar was a pebble's throw away, the gap too far to jump.

How did she get up here?

I stared for a long time at the giant stones. Slowly a long narrow staircase appeared through the gloom. It wound from the ground up the big rock across from me. At the top, there was a plank long enough to bridge the distance from the rock to the door. She must have been positioning it across the gap by herself.

Dawn was breaking, and she would arrive soon. I had to act. I reached below the doorway's edge, feeling sheer cliff below me. The craggy rock had some crevices that could be used as handholds to climb down, but it was too dark to see to the bottom, and I was in no condition to attempt it blindly.

She appeared at the bottom of the stairs, carrying her caldron and basket. I should have waited to chew through the restraints until I was stronger. As soon as she saw I was free, she would subdue and tie me again—using iron instead of leather this time.

Surprise was my only weapon now. I had only one option and little time.

I dragged myself back, grunting and wrenching myself onto the pallet. I pulled the fur cover completely over me. The Raven hooted and jumped from the window to the altar. I ignored her, gathering my feeble energy.

I heard her position the plank in the door, and I feigned sleep. Her footsteps crossed the plank and approached the pallet. The Raven screeched, alerting her that something was wrong, but it was too late to alter my plan. I only had one chance.

I gritted my teeth and lunged at her, reaching for the sword sheathed at her side. My left hand grasped the pommel, and I managed to draw the blade. It was heavy, and I swung wildly, without strength or control. She took a small step back. The sword dropped from my hand and crashed to the floor. I collapsed, panting, helpless and grasping my throbbing belly.

She had needed neither strength nor magic to defeat me. She plucked up the sword and sheathed it at her side, smirking. The Raven cackled.

"What will you do now, Gerwulf?"

# Strength of a Wulfhedinn

~~~~

She did not tie me up again but simply let me rest. When I was ready, she tried to help me sit up.

I pulled out of her arms. "Leave me."

She sat back, her sword within my reach. She obviously had no fear of me. I pushed myself up slowly with my uninjured arm and braced myself against the wall.

"You chewed through the straps quickly," she said. "How far did you get last night? All the way to the door?"

I glared at her, so clever and smug. They saw everything, she and her all-seeing Raven. I despised them both.

"The door then," she said. "Good. It will get easier every time, but now you must eat." She reached for her caldron.

"I told you, no more of your poison!" I seethed.

She set the warm pot in my lap and took off the iron top. The aroma of roasted meat filled the air. My mouth watered.

"Rabbit and carrots—no potions," she said, pulling a flagon

from a basket. "And there is bread, cheese and beer."

I grabbed the meat with my fingers, smelled it, and touched it to my tongue. It tasted clean, so I gorged, washing it down with the beer.

"I need more," I said between gulps of meat and beer— gone within moments.

"Much more." She nodded. "But it will take time to regain the strength you had."

I wiped the pot clean with the bread and devoured it with the cheese. I belched. Seasoned with hunger, it was the best meal I ever had—better than the King's feast.

"Why did you not let me die?" I asked. "Why have you brought me here? I know where I am—at the Raven's Stones— and you are a Saxon."

"So many questions. You must be feeling better." She grinned. "Let me check your wounds. It is probably time to pull out the stitches."

Despite the weakness, I was feeling better. She unwrapped the dressings on my arm and leg. They had stayed dry without bleeding for days now.

She pulled out a small pair of snips. "This will not hurt un- less you move and cause me to stab you," she warned. "And I *will* stab you if I must."

"I have been sewn before," I said.

Starting on my arm, she cut the stitches and pulled out the threads one by one. Her steady fingers moved with skill, her face serious and focused. She bit the corner of her lip as she worked, taking care not to cause me pain.

Her warm touch gently tugged, snipped, and pulled each thread. They slid smoothly through my skin, a strangely relax- ing sensation. After she had pulled the last stitch out of my arm, she rubbed the scabbing wound with ointment and massaged the muscles around it. My head rolled back against the wall…her scent close, mingling with mine.

*…Sweet musk and hawthorn…*

"I remember you," I said.

"Yes?" She continued to rub my arm.

"You wear the face of the Raven. You rode with the rebel Widukind and tried to run me down in the forest—twice. You were with the Wulfhednar when they attacked me."

She paused and replied, "It took great magic—and great force—to take you, and it will take much to restore you."

"Why would you do that?"

She drew away the fur, and I forgot my question when she bent over the stitches on my bare thigh. Her hair tumbled down and brushed my loins. She moved closer, and her sheathed sword shifted within my reach. She seemed unaware of it as she snipped and pulled the stitches. Engrossed in her task, her back to me, she was vulnerable.

A few moments ago, I was angry and foolish enough to grab the sword and wrench her to the ground by her hair. Now, lulled by her touch and the gentle tugging and pulling of the stitches, I reached for her hair and touched a glossy tendril. It felt so soft between my fingers.

She peered over her shoulder, glancing at my hand, my crotch, and the sword. She returned to the stitches. She was unafraid of me, yet I sensed something else in her manner. Trust? Or arrogance? No one dared turn their back on me, but I let her care for me, and she finished too soon.

"Your muscles are still binding together, but you can start

working them," she said. "Later today, after you sleep a bit."

"I will start now," I said, feeling strengthened by the hearty meal.

"You are not as strong as you believe." She shook her head. "You will mend, but to become the man you once were, you must have patience."

She gingerly touched my eyelid and stroked the battered cheek and jaw below it. "The swelling is much improved. I can almost see what you look like." She smiled. "Now, I must clean your belly. Lay back."

I eased myself down and suppressed a groan, hating that she saw me wince.

She began to peel off the bandage, watching my reaction. I jerked up and grabbed her arm, stifling a cry.

She put a gentle hand on mine and said, "I can give you the potion."

"No," I grunted. "Do it now."

"As you wish."

I took several deep breaths, and she stripped it off with one gesture. I saw the wound for the first time without the effects of the potion. It was a cavern—an injury I would not expect a man to survive. But despite the size, it was healing cleanly now, without pus, filling with shiny new flesh, pink and tender like suckling pig's. It would take a long time for it to close and longer to build the strength to swing a sword or throw an axe—if it was possible at all.

"The gods were with you," she said. "It is deep, but it missed your entrails or large veins. It festered, but someday, you will have great strength and fight as you once did."

She knew everything, saw everything—read my thoughts. I despised her again, for the power she held over me, for my weakness…because I lived yet was hardly alive, little more than a living corpse. I gritted my teeth while she rinsed the wound. I trembled as sweat ran down my face and body, and I fought to stay conscious.

She stopped working. "You have grown pale. Rest for a moment," she said gently.

"Finish it," I gasped.

With a nod, she applied new ointment and a fresh bandage. I had to rest before trying to move again—but I would show her the strength of a Wulfhedinn…later…someday.

# Become as You Are

〜〜〜

I dozed through the morning and awoke renewed. It was less difficult to push myself up and move. In the corner, there was a pot to shit in, and the witch had left a flagon, a cup, and a thick slice of bread and cheese on the stone altar across the room. I was famished and wished she had left them within reach, next to the pallet. I would have to brace myself along the wall to help support my injured leg to get there. She was clever, forcing me to work to get there. It seemed so far until I saw the crutch next to the pallet.

I stood, bracing the wooden crutch under my uninjured arm, and hobbled across the room. There was no magic in it, but it worked well enough. The trip was tiring but easier than crawling or walking along the wall.

With every step, I imagined how good the beer would taste. My mouth watered for it, driving me forward, but I found that she had left me water—not beer. It quenched my thirst well enough and helped wash down the bread and cheese.

The Raven flew in the little window and perched. I hobbled around on the crutch, and her head rotated as I limped back and forth.

I tired and rested on the pallet. "Does she come soon?" I asked the Raven. "I need food."

She bobbed her head and flew off.

I ached for the time when I could move with more strength. I wanted to throw the crutch out the door and force myself to walk without it, but I had to concede that I needed it now. I had suffered many injuries before but none had crippled me so seriously. None had brought me as close to death. It would take time, as the witch had said, and I despised her for it.

I began to move and bend my injured arm. It was sore, but it felt good to force usefulness into it. I wondered if I would ever have the strength to wield a long axe again.

Many of my bruises had disappeared except the largest ones, fading into shades of green and yellow. I rose again with the crutch and paced across the floor. My balance was better this time. By the time she and the Raven returned, I had crossed the room a dozen times and shit in the pot.

"It is good to see you up, and your color is better. Work and pain suit you."

I scoffed, dropping in exhaustion onto the pallet. "I am starving."

"I imagine you are."

She brought more roasted meat and vegetables, beer, bread, and cheese. I ate like a king and thought that she must be of high standing to have such food. I wondered why she would feed it to me.

She pulled a pair of linen breeches and a belt from the basket. "I brought these for you, now that you can dress yourself."

"You mean, now that I do not have to shit myself," I replied.

It proved challenging to pull up breeches with a lame leg and bad arm, another indignity. I adapted, adjusting so that my strong arm performed most of the simple task. Covering my nakedness rekindled a sense of power.

She had brought more water and a small basin. "You can do your own bathing as well and rub your muscles with this ointment several times a day, but do not touch your belly wound," she directed. "I will see to that—if you want it to heal properly."

"Why do you tend me so well?" I asked.

She touched my wounded arm. "You have been on your own for too long."

"I am a Christian and a Frank—your enemy." I let her hand rest there for a moment then pulled away from her. "I had set out against you, against your leader. You should have killed me."

"I do not kill Wulfhedinn."

"Why do you keep me prisoner here?"

She threw back her long hair and laughed. "Where else would you go? You can barely walk to the door."

"I *will* be strong again—soon. Will you leave the bridge in the door for me then?"

"Yes," she said.

She surprised me, but I sensed there was more left unsaid.

"You will simply let me go?"

She walked over to the little window and peered out. "On the day that the sun rises highest in the sky, I will let you go. You will descend from Wodan's tower and will become as you are."

"I am ready now!"

She smirked, keeping secrets in her red lips and deep eyes.

She left, leaving the door open but withdrawing the bridge before I could hobble there. By the time I reached it, she had descended a long way down the winding stairway.

"What do you want?!" My voice echoed off the giant stones, but she did not look up. "What do you want of me?" I called again.

# A Powerful Vengeful God

~~~~

She returned morning, noon, and evening with untainted food and fresh water, as she had promised. She stood at the little window every morning while I ate.

I could only see the tops of trees and sky through the window. "What do you stare at?" I asked between bites of food.

"The dawn," she replied.

She cleaned my gut and applied fresh ointment and linen. It was the worst part of the day, but the wound continued to heal, and the pain gradually lessened. In the afternoons, she pushed me longer and faster. I spent the time between her visits pacing, massaging my muscles, and planning for the day when I would be strong.

I thought of Pyttel, the strange, mad monk. He claimed that I had redeemed myself by returning the Holy Spear to the King. He had released me from excommunication, and the King had bestowed a title of honor on me—Royal Scout and

Huntsman. I had been given the name Tracker, been shaved and shorn, and sworn my oath of fealty.

That was a long time ago: many weeks, a couple of months? I scratched my chin, fully covered again with a long beard, wild and unruly. God would not recognize me, and without my cross, He would not hear my prayers. I was more alone than I had ever been. During the long hours, I began to look forward to the witch's visits more than her poisoned broth.

After several more days, I could limp half a dozen paces without the crutch before collapsing.

The next time she returned, I waited just inside door while she climbed the stairs. She lifted the heavy plank and set it across the gap. I surprised her without the crutch, taking a step onto the narrow plank. She stepped hard on it, causing it to bounce. My weak leg quivered and threatened to collapse and toss me to the ground far below. I threw myself back into the chamber.

When she reached the door, I flung the crutch at her. It missed and flew through the door, tumbling down the rock face. I heard it splinter against the stone and hit the ground.

"You are not ready yet," she said.

"I am ready enough! Let me go or kill me!"

"I will keep you for now," she said.

"Why? Why do you keep me like a prisoner here?"

She set down the caldron and basket and said, "Teach me the prayers of your god—the Christian magic."

I tried to rise and fell again. "My prayers have no magic."

She stood over me. "Do you think that because the blood of the Wulfhedinn runs in your veins?" she asked. "The forces you invoke are powerful. It frightens Christians enough to cast you out, then your king chooses to take you back—to use you for his own purposes."

"God Himself damned me," I said.

"Did he?" She tilted her head.

"What would you know of it?" She was trying to trick me with her words, and I refused to speak to her the rest of the day.

That night I tossed on my pallet, trying to push her out of my head. I did not sleep until close to dawn. When I woke, she was leaning on the little window, resting her cheek in her hand. The Raven alighted and perched on her arm. She cooed to it and stroked it with a gentle touch. She leaned out the window. Her unbound hair fell over her shoulders, and the sunshine lit her fair face, crowning her and the Raven in light. She was different, standing in the sun.

*Angel and white dove*
*Eyes of heaven*
*Holy Spirit in her palm*
*All that is good and pure*
*All that is right*
*Mother*

"Hail Mary, full of grace..." The words flowed from my mouth before I could stop them.

"What is it you say?" She leaned in from the window. "A Christian prayer?"

I had not said the prayer but once since my mother had died, but the words were warm and familiar, and the angel beckoned me to finish. "...the Lord is with thee. Blessed art thou among women, and blessed is the fruit of thy womb."

Her face glowed. "It is beautiful."

"...a prayer to the Holy Mother of God's Son, the Lord Jesus Christ," I said softly.

"Mary is your god's lover?" Her voice rang with innocence,

seeking to understand.

"No. She is a virgin."

"A virgin?" she mused. "A maiden who birthed a god? She must be a powerful goddess. I thought Christians worshipped no goddesses."

"She is not a goddess but a saint."

"A saint?"

"One who lives piously and ascends into heaven to be with God."

*She releases the dove*
*It soars, snowy wings splinter to black*
*Blocking the sun*
*Shadow and darkness...*
*Raven and witch*
*Eater of Souls*

She watched the Raven ascend. "Your saints are like our warriors who fight bravely and travel to Walhalla to be with Wodan in his great hall."

"Murderous warriors are not like saints!" I thrust myself upright and fell back.

"Warriors of Wodan fight valiantly and die in battle with honor—they are the Chosen Ones." She strode to the edge of my pallet, hands on hips. "Only *your* god sees you as murderous. He is a powerful, vengeful God. See what he has done to you?"

I rolled away from her, my wounds throbbing. Her probing eyes burrowed into my scarred back, wounding me worse than a lashing.

"Give me the prayer of your mighty Father God," she said.

"I will give you nothing," I said.

# The Witch's Promise

Days passed. The witch attended me, but we spoke no more of Christian prayers or heathen gods. She checked my belly wound and left food and water. Her visits were uncomfortably silent, and the time alone was endless.

I stood at the door and windows for hours, observing the area around the giant stones. There were a small meadow and a stream that filled a pool next to the stones. Beyond that, the thick forest enclosed the area.

The only one I had seen was the witch until one afternoon when a dozen warriors arrived and set up camp around the stones. They wore wolf skins—Saxon Wulfhednar.

They were well-equipped, each with a long sword, a seax, and a dagger, as well as spears and francisca axes. They patrolled the area and spent hours training and working to build strength. The sounds of grunting and weapons hitting shields echoed up the rock to me. They laughed heartily and drank together in the evenings with one voice, one heart—theirs was a pack that lived and hunted together.

They did not look up at me, although I stood at the door and window within clear sight. I did not exist to them.

I smelled Widukind among the warriors, but I was too high above them to see faces clearly or hear their conversations; only their laughter was loud enough for me to hear up in the tower.

One warrior stood out from the others—the largest of them all. He was broad and strong and followed by several others. He was the most was sought after, the most followed, the most respected—the leader Widukind.

Large groups of peasant farmers soon came to train with his warriors. None of them had armor or swords, and they were more adept at archery than at fighting. They hunted with bow and arrow to supplement the food they raised, and most had excellent aim. Working together proved more challenging. They broke into two groups, lined up behind straw barriers, and practiced standing together and shooting. Sometimes, one or two would jump up and shoot too early, giving away their position. When it happened, others dropped their bows and jumped them, beating them with their fists. Soon, it happened no longer.

The farmers also practiced with axe and spear under direction of the warriors. They also wrestled and exercised to build strength. Skinny untrained peasants transformed into strong, deft fighters. Over the weeks, I counted several thousand recruits—the makings of a large rebel army.

I became more determined to find a way down. I studied the rock cliff outside the door and the arched window. I felt for cracks in which I could hook my hands. There were some good handholds, but no clear way to climb down. My best option was to wait until I could overpower the witch and cross the bridge, which was straining my patience. I would also have to avoid the warriors. I could not possibly fight them all.

I observed their movements, trying to determine where they went and when, but there were no clear patterns. More peasants arrived frequently. They pitched camp, trained and were replaced with more peasants. They must have used a safe passageway through the treacherous forest to get there, but they emerged like ghosts from the dense trees.

I began to work on building my own strength, following their training. I squatted and stood, and pushed my weight up from the floor with my arms. My limbs quivered and would not perform the tasks, no matter how determined I was.

The witch stood silently as I worked, then one afternoon she frowned and said, "You are pushing too hard." They were the first words she had spoken since we talked of God. "If you rush healing, you will only slow it down. You must allow the muscles enough time to bind together, or you will tear them apart again."

Her voice irritated me, and I rejected all she said. I was Wulfhedinn. I was ready.

I pushed myself off the floor from my stomach, up and down, until sweat poured from my body and my arms screamed for relief. The arm that had been slashed quivered, but I continued to push on until something tore. I collapsed onto my gut, unable to suppress a moan.

"There now. You have torn the wound on your arm, and it's bleeding again," she said without trying to help me.

I wiped away the blood. "It is nothing," I said.

"Now you must start all over with that arm," she said. "You must learn to rely on your healthy side, and increase the work on the weak side slowly and steadily."

"Stop badgering me!"

She laughed. "Your eyes are so dark when you are angry with me," she said. "Did you know that they turn green when you smile? I hope to see them green again soon."

I would give her no such satisfaction that day. I kept a determined scowl on my face over the next couple of weeks. Slowly, my weak arm improved until I could push myself off the floor without collapsing.

"It would have come much faster if you had let it heal properly," she said.

I could take it no longer. "I will do this my way!"

"Yes, you will."

The next morning, she carried a large object and climbed the steps more slowly than usual. When she reached the top, her face was red, and sweat rolled off her forehead. She breathed heavily and set a heavy bench and her basket at my feet. The basket fell over, and several large stones of various sizes rolled out.

"Use these stones to build your strength," she said, "but if you turn them on me, you will regret it. And this bench is not for sitting. Step on and off it to prepare your legs to descend the staircase."

"Descend the stairs? When will that be?"

"Soon."

My limp was almost gone, but it was difficult to step on the bench with my weak leg—far harder than I expected. I started lifting the smaller stones to the side and overhead to strengthen my arms. At first, I had to hold my abdomen for support, but it gradually got used to the strain. I worked up to the larger stones until I dropped one, barely missing my head.

The witch smirked. It was almost worse than her badgering.

When she left, I returned to lifting smaller stones. The routine became easier over a few days. I soon gained some weight. My skin no longer hung on me like an old man's; it had filled out with lean muscle, and my ribs were less visible.

One afternoon, she brought two wooden staffs. She tossed one to me and hoisted the other in a well-practiced stance.

"I will not hurt you," she said with an elusive smile.

*The wolf snapped*
*Impatient to pounce…*
*Attack*

She immediately whacked my knuckles. I dropped the staff, feeling the sting in my pride more than my hand.

"A Wulfhedinn does not make such mistakes," she said.

My face burned. I had let her bait me. How could I be such a fool? Had I forgotten everything? She would not see my weaknesses again.

We worked every day. She disarmed me often and had the strength to take me down, but she held back. She only attacked my strong side and avoided the gut. I hated it and waited for the day she made a mistake and lowered her defense. I whacked her hard in the shoulder and knocked her down. It must have stung fiercely, but she did not show it.

The small victory did not feel good. I lowered my staff, and reached to help her up, but she scrambled to her feet by herself.

"You are ready for swords now," she said.

She meant wooden swords—another humiliation.

"They are children's toys," I protested.

"You do not want me to pull steel on you yet," she said.

The sword and shield she gave me were weighted—twice the weight of real weapons. I could barely lift the sword with my injured arm.

"Too heavy?" She smirked. "A child could lift it."

"I want to train with an axe."

"Swords are not so different," she said. "Keep moving. Attack quickly. Defend and counterattack more quickly."

I knew this and hated to be reminded of it as though I were a child.

We sparred every day with the swords and shields. My grip was getting stronger, and she did not disarm me again, but she was holding back. I hated it.

After one long afternoon of training, she lunged with abrupt force. I turned the blow with my shield, but her strength knocked me down.

"That is enough for today," she said.

"No!" I fumed, rising.

I thrust my weighted sword at her heart. She blocked it and struck me down again with a quick counterblow on my injured arm. My groan filled the room before I could stifle it.

"You have the head of a bull—like your father," she said, "but you do not have his strength yet."

"What would you know of my father?" I seethed.

"You are half-Saxon, are you not? A bastard."

I picked myself off the floor again. "My father was a beast that raped my mother, cursing us both for the rest of our lives," I said. "That is what *I* know."

"That is the story many Franks know. Life would have been worse for you both had the truth been known," she said.

"What truth?"

"—that your mother loved the Saxon Wulfhedinn, and he her."

*Father...Mother*
*She walks through the woods*

*Drawn to the blue glow*
*…the sacred spring*
*The little boy creeps behind*
*From the shadows*

*She strips her tunic, white skin radiant in the Wodan's light*
*She chants and sacrifices to Virgin Mary, Great Mother*
*Her offerings and her naked body please Wodan*
*Bathing in his warm waters*
*Glistening on her pale skin*

I thought of how beautiful my mother had been in the waters of the spring, and how they flowed gracefully over the rock wall. I had heard that the ancient peoples, the ancestors of both Frank and Saxon, had built the wall to contain the sacred waters and make a pool where the Eye of Wodan could dwell.

One day on the way home from the spring, my mother had called to me.

"Gerwulf, come out now." She spoke with great foreboding, knowing all along that I followed her. "You must not return to the spring or tell anyone what you have seen there."

"Why?" I asked although I would not have spoken of it. I wanted the mysteries of the sacred spring to be something that only we shared.

"There has been a great war, and our King has won a victory over the heathen Saxons." She frowned, and there was sadness in her voice.

"We have won?"

"Yes—and no," she said. "Many of the Saxon leaders have renounced Wodan and the old gods and accepted Christian baptism."

"But that is good...they believe in Jesus now."

"Yes, but you must understand...the strength and fury of Wodan are strong in you. You see in the night. You are stronger and run faster than a grown man and frighten boys twice your size. As a toddling boy, you had the battle rage, like a beast. Others see it too, the mark of the Wulfhedinn, a warrior of Wodan."

"Am I evil?"

"No, you are blessed—by both gods, but it is no longer safe to worship both old and new gods. The warriors of the Christian God are defeating those of Wodan. You must be steadfast in your worship of the One True God. Wear your cross—always."

"I will, Mama."

*She reaches to embrace the boy in her bosom*
*...gone before I feel her touch*
*Alone in a cold stone tower*
*Her face fades from memory*
*Maybe not to return again*

The chamber was dead silent. The witch was gone, but I longed to see her, to feel her touch. I needed her to care for me, to fight me, and to defeat me. I went to the door and glimpsed her as she reached the bottom of the stairs. I almost called for her to return but held my tongue.

I ripped the dressing off my belly, grimacing as it tore at the raw flesh. I picked up a large stone and heaved it high in the air over my head until my arms ached...until sweat washed away the tears.

*Sorrow runs deeper than any wound*
*I want her to come back*

When she returned in the evening, I was soaked with sweat and exhausted.

"I thought you might be extra hungry." Her gaze lingered on my chest, pumping with every breath I took. "I brought twice the meat, cheese, and bread."

She opened the lid, and I could not resist the aroma of roasted meat. I dropped the big stone and sat on the bench. I ate greedily, washing the meal down with beer.

"So you have not learned to use a cup yet?" she asked.

"Bring me more beer," I grunted wiping my mouth with the back of my hand.

"More beer would cloud your mind," she reminded me. "Drink water."

She was badgering me again. I chugged the water, glaring at her between every swallow.

"You were going to hit me with that stone?" she asked.

I gulped several more mouthfuls before answering. "I thought better of it."

"Perhaps, then, you are redeemable," she said.

I slammed down the flagon, cracking it and breaking off the handle.

She took no notice of it. "Your Frankish king has tried to drive out the old gods for more than a decade, but now we have you. Your redemption is not in heaven. It is here—with us."

"I am your enemy. I was sent by King Karl to track down your leader, Widukind!"

"Yes, but in the end, your fool king only sent you to us. To-morrow, you will understand."

I had enough of her riddles and being her prisoner in the stone tower. I jumped up and grabbed a long staff, ready to overcome her. I was strong enough now—I was Wulfhedinn. She could no longer stop me, and she knew it. I saw it on her face.

She swung her leg over the bench and straddled it. Raising her arms, she made herself vulnerable, daring me to swing at her.

"Leave now, if that is what you want." She nodded toward the door. "But your King and his court will treat you like the animal they believe you to be."

Her cleverness enraged me. I slammed the staff against my thigh, snapped it in half, and threw it out the door.

She leaned forward and said, "Wait...one more day." She spoke to me like a comrade. "If you want to go back to the Frankish king tomorrow, I will give you your skin and axes and let you go."

I went to the door, scanning the ground below. The warriors and the peasant soldiers had broken camp and left, and the area lay deserted. I looked back at her and saw no deceit in her shining face. I swallowed hard, considering the witch's promise.

"One more day," I said.

# Chooser of the Living and the Slain

‡

I rocked gently in sleep. Something was beating outside, inside…inside me…a low thump…a warm pulse, soothing me with endless rhythm. It came from within and without, carrying me backward and onward. The deep tempo carried me into a profound sleep, aware, yet blissfully free of thought.

> *Beating…beating…beating*
> *Faint, growing louder*
> *Beating…beating…beating*
> *Slow growing faster*
> *Beating…beating…beating*
> *Faster*
> *Louder*
> *Nearer*

I smelled a storm. Lightning struck, and thunder boomed, shaking the stone walls. My heart hammered in its cage. Blood surged through my body, kindling fire.

*Beating...beating...beating*

The Raven shrieked, and she stood before me, alight by fire bolts that struck inside the chamber. Her beak and red eyes drew close, threatening to devour me.

*Beating...beating...beating*

Her feathers glistened, wings spreading to engulf me, to carry me away.

*Beating...beating...beating*

She vanished, feathers falling to the ground, revealing a woman of flesh and blood. I was awake, and she was here, the witch.

*Beating...beating...beating*

An army of booming drums drove the storm away, and the moon came out. Her naked body swayed with the beating, washed in silver streaks of moonlight. The light danced across her breasts and shimmered across waves of long black hair. She twirled close to me, her tresses twirling then falling to brush my bare skin.

*Beating...beating...beating*

The din drove her dance wilder, ecstatic and forceful. She reeled and lurched, and my heart surged, igniting my body.

*I am Vala, warrior, healer, and the Chooser of the Living and the Slain. I am Walkyrie, and I chose you for life.*

"Why do you want me?" My voice quivered.

*Her lips brush my ear, a whisper, an echo*

*Primal, raw…passionate*
*You are Wulfhedinn*
*You are Gerwulf*

*Beating…beating…beating*

Her legs gripped me as she danced. I clutched her thighs, feeling powerful bands of muscle as she thrust upon me. She lurched, and I plunged deeper and deeper.

*Beating…beating…beating*
*Louder*
*Faster*
*Beating…beating…beating*

I shuddered, crashing into oblivion.

# Into the Raven's Night

It was morning, bright and fresh.

...sweet musk and hawthorn...her scent lingered on me, the scent of arousal.

She stood at the little window wearing a thin linen gown. A small ray of sun streamed through the window and shone through the fabric, draping over her breasts and buttocks. Her hair hung loosely around her shoulders, crowned by a ring of dripping white flowers—hawthorn. She turned toward me. She was Vala, and today she would fulfill her promise.

So much was different—this woman, me. She bore no weapons, and for a moment, all thoughts of leaving vanished next to the beauty of her body.

She lifted a silver cup and smiled. "Gerwulf, rise and come here."

I joined her at the little window. She stepped away from the light, and it fell against the wall in the shape of an arrow.

"Watch it as the sun rises higher," she said.

The arrow of light moved across the wall slowly.

"It points to you." Her eyes met mine.

The arrow continued to move until it lit up the stone man—my prison guard. Bathed in sun, his fearsome expression became joyous.

"You are free!" she declared. "It is midsummer, the day you will descend the stairs, Gerwulf. Today is special, and we drink mead."

I now understood her vigil at the little window every dawn. She had measured the progress of the sun as it rose. This morning, it reached its highest point so that its rays shone through the little round window. It was midsummer now, but why had she waited for this day to set me free?

She lifted the goblet in a toast and drank deeply and handed it to me. The mead smelled of honey. I finished it, feeling its spirit warm my throat.

I reached for my breeches, but she put her hand on my arm and stopped me. She crowned my head with a circlet of hawthorn like her own. It was free of thorns…the aroma of sweet musk and dripping white flowers was almost overwhelming.

She took me by the hand and led me through the door and across the narrow bridge. I stood free of the stone tower for the first time. The midsummer sun warmed my face, and I took a deep breath of fresh air. I wanted to make the trip down the stairs last a long time. At the same time, I wanted to hurry, to have my feet touch the earth as soon as possible.

We descended, circling around the massive rock until we reached the bottom. She led me gently past the other giant stones toward the pond. We passed more chambers carved into the rocks, like caves. They appeared empty. We were alone.

At the water's edge stood a huge boulder. An arched alcove was carved into the rock, and within the recess lay a hole shaped like a man—a dead man with his arms folded across the chest. I stopped to stare at it, shivering at the memory.

"Come now. Forget that place." Vala pulled me playfully toward her. "It is a place for the dead, but today you are free and very much alive!"

She laughed and dropped her gown on the bank of the pool. The sunshine sparkled on the waters, sacred waters, reflecting a perfect blue from the heavens. Wodan was present, but now I was not afraid. It was a morning different than all others.

Vala slipped into the pool and dove under, reappearing far from the bank. I followed and plunged in. The cool water flowed across my skin and through my hair and beard, washing away the filth and sweat of months of healing. I pumped my arms and legs, propelling through the water...strong and without pain.

*Sacred blue waters*
*Alive, yet in heaven*

I came up for air and saw that Vala had swum farther away. She laughed and splashed at me. I swam toward her, but she stayed out of reach, giggling.

"Your eyes are as green this morning as the summer grass," she said.

I was smiling and laughing. It had been a long, long time...

I reeled, flooded with joy. I swam after her again, but she vanished under the water every time I came near. We played this game until I was exhausted, gasping for breath and laughing at the same time.

She dove again, this time disappearing for a long time. I scanned the surface, eager for her to reappear. I saw no sign of her. Moments passed, and she did not emerge.

"Vala!" I called.

No answer, so I shouted louder, searching for a ripple that would mark her place in the water. Our flowery crowns floated, locked together.

Suddenly, her hands were running up my thighs to my cock. Then she gripped my ass and burst out of the water, sliding her body against mine.

"You called for me." Her hair and eyelashes glistened with droplets.

I ached to have her as she was this moment, stripped of all darkness, radiant in the sun—a woman. I drew her nearer, and she pressed against me, her wet lips meeting mine. I drank in the taste of her.

*Sweet musk and hawthorn*

I clutched her to my heart. Her strong hands gripped my chest and shoulders fiercely, then her fingers ran down my arms softly, and she took my hand.

"Come." She guided me out of the pool. "It is time."

I wanted to taste more of her. Without thought, I followed. As we neared the water's edge, a reflection of a wolf appeared in the gently lapping ripples. I pulled back; was it me? I did not want to wear the wolf mask today.

A huge wolf stood on the bank of the pool. How long had it been there? Another wolf appeared then another. More came until a pack of a dozen surrounded the pond.

I pulled Vala back, shielding her.

"Do not fear them," she said. "They have not come to attack; they are here to welcome you."

Confused, my head was spinning. Vala's touch on my hand reassured me, and she guided me out of the water. I followed her as if I had no will at all. On the bank, the ground wavered under my feet, and I stumbled and fell to my knees.

Drums were pounding. When had they started again?

*Beating…beating…beating*
*Faint, growing louder*
*Beating…beating…beating*
*Slow growing faster*
*Beating…beating…beating*
*Faster*
*Louder*
*Nearer*

The wolves drew together, forming a tight circle around us. They grew larger and more fearsome as each drumbeat struck.

*Beating…beating…beating*
*Faster*
*Louder*
*Harder*

Their jaws opened impossibly wide, and their fangs grew grotesque and sharp. They spun around me, prancing and pouncing on invisible prey to the beat. They howled and raged and stood on two legs, revealing weapons and shields like men. The frenzy escalated, and they snarled and snapped and banged their shields with swords and spears.

*Wulfhedinn*

I rose and faltered again, grabbing for Vala's hand, but she was gone, and the circle of beasts closed in around me.

*Spinning...reeling*
*Beating...beating...beating*
*Faster*
*Louder*
*Harder*

I was lifted to my feet and carried into the circle of wolves. I danced with them, falling and rising, throughout the rest of the day. Midsummer, the longest day. I danced with elation and power, my mind churning in a haze, seeing only wolves. We howled and danced together until I was beyond exhaustion, beyond thought, beyond my body.

At dusk, a great fire was lit. It signaled to the Raven, and she answered from above.

*I hunger*

*Feed the wolf*
*Feed the Raven*

Her shadow covered the giant stones, bringing night. The circle of wolves widened, and she alighted next to me. She rose above me, wearing the Raven's mask and the mantle of black feathers.

*Sweet musk and hawthorn*

*Eyes of fiery blood*
*Eater of Souls*
*Walkyrie*

The drums and dancing stopped, but the echo of spirits rang in my ears. The flames of the fire lit her glossy coat. The largest Wulfhedinn in the circle stepped toward me, his face hidden by the wolf's muzzle, yet I recognized him, his scent…

The Walkyrie spoke, "I give you this man, naked and pure" she said. "He survived the Three Days Sleep and was delivered of the phallus of Wodan, the Father, and into the womb of the Great Mother. Today, on this longest of days, he has descended the great pillar that holds up the skies. He is healed. He is re-born. He is Wulfhedinn…Gerwulf, your son."

My senses came alive. That scent…I had tracked it for the King, to capture him, to kill him. Widukind, the rebel Saxon leader.

*My father*

His stance was as broad as his shoulders. He carried a sword as long as any. He spoke with the wolf's tongue. "Today, on the sacred dawn of Midsummer, I am united with my son, my blood."

He held a long axe, a francisca, and a wolf skin—*mine.*

He raised them. "Do you, my blood and Wulfhedinn, accept this wolf skin and these axes as a warrior of Wodan?"

I saw my hand reach out, but it did not feel like my own. I nodded—or did I? Had my head dipped from faintness? Had I shaken it instead?

He handed me the axes and laid the skin on my back then

pulled up the hood. I looked through its eyes, seeing my father for the first time—wolf to wolf.

...a stab in my chest...cut...warm blood flowing, dripping to the ground. I grabbed my side, the blood running on my hand...cut by her sword, her hand.

*My father*

"Let his blood mix with that of all the pack," he said, holding the spear aloft. "Blood brothers, we follow each other into victory against our enemies or to death. We strive to be reborn in Wodan's great hall in Walhalla. We fight with honor and courage, without fear of the fate the Walkyrie chooses."

The drums beat again, and each Wulfhedinn in the pack was cut. We bled and leapt through the fire. The Walkyrie then cut herself and bled with us. She smeared our bodies with blood-soaked mud and warm ashes.

*Beating...beating...beating*
*Faster*
*Louder*
*Harder*
*...from the longest day far into the Raven's night*

# All is Deception

～～～

I awoke on my pallet. My head pounded, and my sight was cloudy. It cleared slowly as I remembered what had happened last night.

I felt the dried blood and the cut on my chest. It was a scratch—but deep enough to leave a mark.

*She had marked me*
*Branded me*
*Witch, Eater of Souls*
*Deceiver*
*Breaker of promises*
*Opening the door*
*Yet ensnaring me with honeyed mead*
*…with her body*

I got up, and the room spun around me. I fell against the wall, holding myself against it until the dizziness passed. The door was open, and the bridge remained in place, ready to cross…

On the altar below the little round window, my axes and wolf skin were laid carefully. She had left them for me—as promised, but how would she deceive me now?

I walked slowly to the window. The meadow was empty but marked by trampled grass and ashes of last night's bonfire.

My path was open and free—it seemed.

She had promised not to poison me again, yet she had held me captive with magic on the day she vowed to let me go. Now she had returned everything to me and left the door wide open—but it was a day too late. How would she trap me now?

The Raven alighted in the window, cawing lowly.

*Don the skin*
*Take the axes*
*You are free*

*Free*

I could think about it no longer. I threw the skin over my shoulders, grabbed my weapons, and strode through the door. She was standing there, waiting for me on the bridge, her sword sheathed at her side.

"Get out of my way, witch," I threatened her with my long axe.

"As you wish." She shrugged her shoulders. "I will not stop you. Let me come across, and you can go."

"Throw down the sword. You have deceived me too many times."

She pulled her sword and flung it off the bridge.

"Nothing is deception here," she said.

"*All* is deception here! You poisoned my mind again...you seduced me..."

"You drank of the honey of the gods! We *all* drank of it... your father, your blood brothers...me. We danced together. We spilled and mixed our blood together with you, as Wulfhednar and Walkyrie."

She walked toward me and pulled down the neck of her tunic, revealing a fresh cut on her breast. "You are one of us." She reached to touch the matching cut on my chest. "You are bound to me, to the pack, by blood, and by will—if it be your will."

Her touch was warm and soothing. Her eyes invited me to stay, to ease my suffering and heal wounds of the past.

*Tempting me*
*The witch, the Devil*

I did not have my cross to hold, to help make me strong. I tightened my grip on my axes and mustered my will, pushing her away. "I am bound to My King and my God."

She curled her upper lip and sneered. "Then you will remain a cursed beast and continue to see yourself as your god sees you."

"I *am* what he sees."

"No! You are Saxon, proud Wulfhedinn, a Chosen One, a Warrior of Wodan, and the son of Widukind."

"Widukind cursed my mother and me!" I said. "He is no father to me. He violated my mother and created me, a despised beast. She knew...she understood. She baptized me and gave me God's cross and forbade me to wear the wolf skin. She feared its magic, knowing what would happen if I did."

"But you wore it anyway."

"I defied her...I used its powers for evil...for vengeance..."

"On those who had humiliated and beaten you! You only sought to restore your honor."

"I wanted to hurt them, and the wolf demon wanted to kill them. I called upon it to chase them, the monks of the monastery who had turned me out. They ran deep into the forest, and I stalked them, one by one, savoring their fear. They panicked, stumbled, and cried out to God in fear. I *loved* the sound of it. I wanted to make their horror last...and I killed one of them."

"The one who flogged you," she said.

"I tore him apart like he had me," I stopped, trying to subdue the feeling of satisfaction it still gave me. "Then I returned to my village, but the warriors cast me out with stones. They would have killed me, but I ran and led them far into the woods until they became lost in the night. I terrorized them as I had the monks, as the wolf demon I am, hungering for their blood... until I heard the screams from the village, smelled the fire..."

My throat tightened. I could not bear to say any more, to let the rest pass through my mind...

*Bury it*
*Hidden from God, hidden from me*

*...but the Raven sees it all*
*She calls for my soul*

"The village, my mother, was left unprotected," I said, "because of the wolf."

"The wolf?" she asked.

I clenched my jaw, suppressing the tears, but they were stronger than any foe I had fought. They ran freely down my cheek, and I choked. "…because of me…"

Had I spoked these words or imagined them? She reached for my hand, but I pulled away.

"I ran back to the village as fast as I could," I said, "but the Saxons had attacked; everything burned. They had dragged my mother from the house…she lay beaten, dead, but they continued to defile her…" My hands covered my eyes. I tried to kick dirt over the image, like the dog I was, but it could no longer be buried. "They called her a whore who slept with both Saxon and Frank, with God and Wodan…where was my father then if he loved her so much? Was he one of *them*?" I tasted the spit on my tongue.

"It was not your father's war band that attacked the village," she said, "and when he heard of it, he ambushed and massacred them all."

I heard her but was not listening. "And where was *I*?" My voice quivered, so hoarse it was barely a whisper. "Calling upon the wolf demon, the Devil, to grant me revenge…to torture and murder those I despised…" My words lay exposed, unfinished, the last begging to be spoken. I wanted desperately to hide behind the wolf mask but was unable to move to pull it over my head. "I am as guilty as any! The Raven knows…she saw it. She came to feast on my mother's flesh and blood and has haunted me ever since."

The Raven screeched and ruffled her feathers.

"The Raven is who you make her," she said. "For me, she is my eyes and ears, a messenger, my companion. For you, she has become that burden which you cannot endure. The Eater of Your Soul."

I refused to look at her as she kept talking.

"You cannot hide from your deeds or from your god under

the wolf hide," she said. "A Wulfhedinn neither needs nor asks the gods for forgiveness. He lives to be the best he can be, for his own honor and that of his own kind. Your god, your heavenly father, has done more than abandon you…he has castrated you." She paused. "Or have you done that to yourself?"

Her words struck me in the gut like a hammer. I could only react. I grabbed her and pressed my axe against her throat.

She stood fearlessly at the edge of my blade. "Return to your Christians, to those that have beaten you, have despised you," she said. "Wear the skin of the wolf in shame. Let it mark you as a captive of your God and your King, knowing that you will forever be damned—you will *never* be one of them."

*Far away, a wolf howls*
*An aching, lonely call*

*Its beating heart steals inside me*
*Peering through the eyes of the beast*
*…pounding harder and harder*
*Muscles surge*
*Strength rules*

"Go! Coward!" she ordered, teetering on the edge of the bridge. Her words cut deeper than any sword could.

*She calls the wolf to resist, to defy*
*To possess her with more strength and power than she can imagine*
*…restrain and keep her…as she had kept me*

I grabbed her from the edge of the bridge and carried her inside. I thrust her upon the altar and ripped open her tunic.

Her pale flesh broke free, strong and challenging. I covered her mouth with mine, tasting her power, drinking of it. She did not fight me; she responded fiercely, her strong muscles clinging to mine.

She ripped off the wolf hood and seized my jaw with both hands. "Show me your face, Gerwulf," she gasped, no longer the shield maiden, the witch, or the Walkyrie of the Raven's Stones. "I need to see you...your face."

*Vala*
*Sweet musk and hawthorn*
*The scent of a woman aroused*
*Crying with desire*
*Her eyes so blue, like Wodan's spring*
*Drawing me into the funnel...*
*Unmasked, naked before her*
*Not as beast, but as man*

*Eater of Souls*
*Beak dripping blood*
*Screeching, calling, commanding...*
*She is master here*

*...and I am still her prisoner*

I wrenched away from her. She reached one hand out to me. I stepped back, her eyes pulling me forward. I resisted and stepped back again, slowly tearing my gaze from hers.

I dropped my weapons and the skin at the base of the altar. The Raven shrieked in the window.

*I hunger*

*Feed the wolf*
*Feed the Raven*

I turned from her and my wolf skin.

*I am no one's captive*
*Not the wolf, the Raven—or her*
*I fight for my soul*

I ran from the stone chamber, crossed the bridge, and put them behind me. My feet sailed over the steps, taking two at a time, around and around the huge stone all the way to the ground. I could feel her watching me from the top, but I did not look up. At the bottom, I slipped into the forest and steeled myself to her call.

*You will return*

Follow Gerwulf's journey in
Book Two of the Wulfhedinn series,
coming soon.